Jessi's Secret Language

**Look for these and other books
in the Baby-sitters Club series:**

THE BABY-SITTERS CLUB

Jessi's Secret Language
Ann M. Martin

AN
APPLE
PAPERBACK

SCHOLASTIC INC.
New York Toronto London Auckland Sydney

For Cary

ISBN 0-590-41586-7

Copyright © 1988 by Ann M. Martin. All rights reserved. Published by Scholastic Inc. APPLE PAPERBACKS and THE BABY-SITTERS CLUB are registered trademarks of Scholastic Inc.

12 11 10 9 8 7 6 5 4   8 9/8 0 1 2 3/9

Printed in the U.S.A.   11

First Scholastic printing, September 1988

The author would like to thank
Patsy Jensen
for her sensitive evaluation
of the manuscript.

CHAPTER 1

I happen to be very good at languages. Once, my family and I went to Mexico on vacation, and during the week we were there, I practically became bilingual. (Which, in case you're not sure, means able to speak two languages really, really well. In this case, English and Spanish.) If I weren't so good at languages, this story might never have happened.

The story also might never have happened if I weren't so good at ballet. If you think about it, ballet is just another kind of language, except that you talk with your body instead of with your mouth. I feel like I'm talking in circles, though, so let me start my story. I'll begin it on the morning of the day I was going to try out for a part in the ballet that my dance school was planning to put on. My family and I had only been living in Stoneybrook, Connecticut, for a few weeks at that time. . . .

I woke up before my alarm went off. I've

always been able to do that. But for some reason, I always set it anyway. Just in case I should have a mental lapse and *not* wake up on time. The reason I get up early is so that I can practice my ballet.

Every morning, I wake up at 5:29, hit the alarm before it can go off and wake everyone else up, chuck my nightgown, and put on my leotard and warm-up stuff. Then I tiptoe down to the basement. No matter how quiet I am, I know Mama always wakes up and listens to me make my way to the basement. That's just the kind of mother she is. I hope she goes back to sleep after she sees that everything is as it should be. But I'll probably never know. Even though she and I are very close (which is how I know she wakes up when I do), I'll probably never ask if she goes back to sleep, and *she* probably doesn't know that I know she wakes up. It's not the kind of thing you need to talk about.

The *barre* in the basement is one of the nice things about moving to Stoneybrook. As I mentioned earlier, we haven't lived here very long. In fact, until we moved, we had lived in a little house on a little street in Oakley, New Jersey. I was born there. Well, not in the *house* — in Oakley General Hospital — but my parents were already living in the house.

Maybe I should tell you a little about my family now. (I'll get back to the *barre* in the basement in Stoneybrook. Really, I will.) Here are the people in my family: Mama; Daddy; my eight-year-old sister, Becca (short for Rebecca); my baby brother, Squirt (whose real name is John Philip Ramsey, Jr.); and me — Jessi Ramsey. I'm eleven, and my full name is Jessica Davis Ramsey.

My family is black.

I know it sounds funny to announce it like that. If we were white, I wouldn't have to, because you would probably *assume* we were white. But when you're a minority, things are different.

Of course, if you could see me, there wouldn't be any question that I'm black. I have skin the color of cocoa — darkish cocoa — soft black hair, and eyes like two pieces of coal. That's how dark brown they are. They're the darkest brown eyes I have ever seen. My sister Becca looks like a miniature version of me, except that her eyes aren't quite as dark. Also, she doesn't have my long, long legs. Maybe that's why she's not a dancer. (Or maybe it's because of her stage fright.) And Squirt looks like, well, a baby. That's really all you can say about him. He's only fourteen months old. (By the way, he got his nickname from the nurses

3

in Oakley General because he was the smallest baby in the hospital. Even now, he's a little on the small side, but he makes up for it by being extremely bright.)

As I said, we used to live in Oakley. I liked Oakley a lot. In our neighborhood were both black families and white families. (Our street was all black.) And Oakley Elementary was mixed black and white. So was my dancing school. My grandparents and a whole bunch of my cousins and aunts and uncles lived nearby. (My best friend was my cousin Keisha. We have the same birthday.)

Then Daddy's company said they were going to give him a big raise and a big promotion. That was great, of course. The only thing was that they also wanted to move him to the Stamford, Connecticut, branch of the company. That's how we ended up here in Stoneybrook. The company found this house for us in this little town. My parents like small towns (Oakley is pretty small), and Daddy's drive to Stamford each morning isn't long at all.

But — I don't think any of us expected the ·one bad thing we found in Stoneybrook: There are hardly any black families here. We're the only black family in our neighborhood, and I am — get this — the only black kid in the whole entire sixth grade at Stoneybrook Middle School. Can you believe it? I can't.

Unfortunately, things have been a little rough for us. I can't tell if some people here really *don't like* black people, or if they just haven't known many, so they're kind of wary of us. But they sure weren't very nice at first. Things are getting better, though. (Slowly.)

Things started getting better for me when I met Mallory Pike. I think she's going to be my new best friend. (Actually, she *is* my new best friend, but I feel funny saying that — like it might hurt Keisha somehow.) Mallory is this really nice girl in my grade who's part of an eight-kid family. And she got me into a group called the Baby-sitters Club, which has been great.

Well, now I'm way, way ahead of myself, so let me get back to the *barre* in the basement. *Barre* is just a fancy French word for "bar." You know, that railing that ballet dancers hold onto when they're practicing their *pliés* and stuff? Our new house is so much bigger than our house in Oakley, and Daddy's job pays so much more money, that he and Mama set up this practice area in the basement for me. It's got mirrors, and a couple of mats (for warm-ups), and of course, the *barre*.

On the morning I've been telling you about,

I practiced in the basement until I heard Mama and Daddy making coffee in the kitchen. That was my clue that it was time to shower and get dressed for school. I kissed my parents good morning, and then ran upstairs. As I passed Squirt's room, I heard him babbling away, so I went inside and picked him up.

"Morning, Squirts," I said as I lifted him from his crib.

"Ooh-blah," he replied. He says only four real words so far — Mama, Dada, ba (we're pretty sure that means bird), and ackaminnie (which we *know* means ice cream). Otherwise, he just makes funny sounds.

I carried Squirt into Becca's room. Becca was still in bed. She has a terrible time waking up in the morning, so I dumped Squirt on top of her. I can't think of a nicer way to wake up than to look into Squirt's brown eyes and hear him say, "Go-bloo?"

Becca began to laugh. She tried to scold me at the same time. "Jessi!" she cried, but she was laughing too hard to sound cross. It's easy for me to make people laugh.

Becca and I got ready for school, and I changed Squirt's diaper. Then the three of us went downstairs and joined Mama and Daddy for breakfast.

Breakfast is one of my favorite times of day.

Another is dinner. This isn't because I like to eat. It's because I like sitting at a table and looking around at my family, the five of us together, joined by something I could never explain but that I can always feel.

"So," said Mama, as soon as we were served and had begun eating, "tryouts today, Jessi?"

"Yup," I replied.

"Are you nervous, honey?"

"The usual, I guess. No — more than the usual. It's not just that I want to be in *Coppélia*. It's also that I don't know how tryouts are going to go at the new school." The ballet school that I got into in Stamford is bigger, more competitive, and much more professional than the one I'd gone to in Oakley. I know I'm a good dancer, but even though I'd auditioned and gotten into the advanced class at the new school, I was feeling sort of insecure. The most I could hope for at the tryouts that afternoon was not to make a fool of myself. I don't plan on becoming a professional ballerina — I just like ballet, and the way I feel when I dance — but still I wanted to do my best at the tryouts.

"What's *Coppélia*?" Becca wanted to know.

"Oh, it's a great ballet," I said with a sigh. "You'll love it. We'll have to go see it, even if I'm not in it. It's a story about a dollmaker

7

named Dr. Coppelius, this really lifelike doll he creates — that's Coppélia — and Franz, a handsome young guy who falls in love with the doll. He sees her from far away and thinks she's real." I realized I was getting carried away with the story, but Becca looked interested, so I continued. "That's not the only problem, though. See, Franz is engaged to Swanilda (she's pretty much the star of the show), and when Swanilda thinks Franz has fallen in love with another woman, she feels all jealous and hurt. After that, the story gets sort of complicated. Swanilda even changes places with Coppélia, and poor Dr. Coppelius thinks his doll has come to life. In the end, everything is straightened out, and Swanilda and Franz get married, just like they'd planned."

"And live happily ever after," Becca added.

Mama and Daddy laughed. And Daddy said to me in his deep voice, "I know you'll do fine this afternoon, baby."

"Maybe," I replied. "We'll see. Thanks, Daddy. I just hope I don't fall over Madame Noelle or crash into a mirror or something."

That time we all began laughing, since I'd never done anything like that and wasn't likely to. I was still nervous, though.

"Okay, girls. Time to get a move on," Mama said a few minutes later.

Becca and I swallowed the last of our breakfasts, flew upstairs, and had a fight over who would get to use the bathroom first. In the end, we went in together and brushed our teeth in record time. Then we began the mad scurry to get out the door and on our way to school. I always think there's not that much to do in order to get ready, but one of us usually loses something, and then Becca gets into a panic about school. (Lots of things about school upset her.)

That morning it was, "Mama, we're having a *spelling* bee today!"

"Becca, you're probably the best speller in your class. Don't worry."

"But I can't get up there in *front* of everyone."

"Think of me," I told her. "Tryouts this afternoon. I have to dance in front of my whole school."

Becca didn't look comforted.

I took her hand and led her out the front door. "Don't forget," I called over my shoulder to Mama. "After ballet I have a meeting of the Baby-sitters Club."

And then Becca and I were off. Our day had begun.

CHAPTER 2

"Hi! Sorry I'm late!"

I start most meetings of the Baby-sitters Club that way because I'm usually rushing to the meetings from either a ballet class or a sitting job. This time I was rushing in from tryouts. They had gone reasonably well, but I wouldn't *really* know how I'd done until my next class.

"That's okay," Kristy Thomas replied. She spoke briskly, but then she smiled at me, so I knew it really was okay.

I sat down next to Mallory Pike, feeling relieved. Mallory and I are the two newest members of the club, so we don't want to upset anybody. Especially Kristy.

Kristy is the president of the club.

Kristy started the club in order to help out parents in the neighborhood who need sitters, and to earn money, of course. But for me, the club has done something else. It has helped to pave my way here in Stoneybrook. I'm meeting lots of people, especially people in my neighborhood, and those people are finding out that I (a black girl) am not scary or awful or anything except just another eleven-year-old kid, who happens to have dark skin. (And who also happens to be a good dancer, a good joke-teller, a good reader, good at languages, and most important, good with children. But a *terrible* letter-writer.)

I think I'm getting ahead of myself again, though. Let me back up and tell you about Kristy, her club, and the rest of its members. For starters, Kristy and all the other girls except Mallory are eighth-graders. Mal and I are not only newcomers to the club, we're lowly sixth-graders. Anyway, as I said, Kristy was the one who began the club. She started it about a year ago when she saw how hard it was for her mom to find a sitter for Kristy's little brother David Michael. Mrs. Thomas was making phone call after phone call and not getting anywhere.

Kristy thought, wouldn't it be great if her mother could make one call and reach a whole lot of sitters at once? So she teamed up with three other girls — Mary Anne Spier, Claudia Kishi, and Stacey McGill — and they formed the Baby-sitters Club. (Stacey's no longer living in Stoneybrook, and Mal and I and another girl, Dawn Schafer, have joined the club, but I'll tell you about all that later.)

Anyway, the club meets on Monday, Wednesday, and Friday afternoons from five-thirty until six. People who need a sitter call us at those times (the club advertises a lot, so our clients know how to reach us), and when they call, they reach *six* sitters! Kristy, Claudia, Mary Anne, Dawn, Mal, and me. They're bound to get a sitter for their kids with just that one phone call.

As president, Kristy keeps the club running very professionally. Long ago, she got a record book in which we write down all sorts of things — our job appointments, of course, plus information about our clients, as well as all the money we earn.

Kristy also makes us keep a club notebook. We're supposed to write about every job we go on. The notebook is a sort of diary telling about which kids we sat for, what went on, how the kids behaved, and any problems we ran into. Once a week, each of us is supposed to read the last week's entries so we can stay on top of things. We all agree that this was a good idea of Kristy's, and that reading the notebook is helpful. But writing about the jobs can be a pain. Oh, well.

I know why Kristy is the president of the

Baby-sitters Club. It's because she's a take-charge kind of person who is brimming with ideas. Kristy's one of those people who's always beginning sentences with, "*I* know, let's . . ." or "Hey, how about . . ." She has a big mouth and loves to be bossy. Some kids don't like her, but I do. I like lively people who surprise you now and then.

Kristy has a mom, two older brothers named Sam and Charlie (they're in high school), and her younger brother David Michael, who's seven. Also, since her mom (who was divorced) got remarried, Kristy now has a stepfather, Watson Brewer, and a little stepsister and stepbrother. Karen is six and Andrew is four. (Kristy's father left the Thomases a long time ago, and Kristy hardly ever hears from him.)

Kristy used to live right across the street from Claudia Kishi (we hold our club meetings in Claudia's bedroom) and next door to Mary Anne Spier, but when her mother and Watson got married, the Thomases moved across town to Mr. Brewer's mansion. (He's a millionaire or something.) Kristy's having sort of a hard time adjusting to her new rich neighborhood (boy, can I relate to that), but she still sees her old friends, the club members. We use part of our club dues to pay Kristy's brother Charlie to drive her to and from Claudia's house so that she never has to miss a meeting. Plus, she still goes to Stoneybrook Middle School, and she and Mary Anne are still best friends. (They had lived next door to each other since they were babies.)

Kristy has brown hair, brown eyes, and is on the small side. She *always* dresses in jeans, turtlenecks, sweaters, and sneakers, and she has no interest at all in boys. She thinks they are gigantic pains. (So do I.)

The vice-president of the club is Claudia Kishi. This is mostly because Claudia has a private phone and private phone number, so it's very convenient to hold our meetings in her room. When job calls come in, they don't tie up anyone else's line. (Once Mal and I tried to start a baby-sitting club of our own at her house, but her brothers and sisters always wanted to use the phone, so that never worked out. Also, our club needed some older members, not just us two sixth-graders.) But when Claudia's phone rings during a meeting, we can be pretty sure it's a job call.

Claudia is absolutely the most exotic, sophisticated thirteen-year-old I have ever seen. She's Japanese-American, and has long, silky, black hair which I don't think I've ever seen her wear the same way twice. She braids it, puts it in ponytails, winds it around her head, and decorates it with clips or ribbons or barrettes or scarves or whatever she feels like. Her eyes are almost as dark as mine and she has a complexion I once heard Kristy say she would kill for (not that there's anything wrong with Kristy's skin). And her clothes! You should see Claudia's clothes. Mallory and I have talked about her outfits. Claudia wears things our mothers won't let us wear until we're forty-five, if then. Don't get me wrong. Her clothes aren't, like, revealing or anything. It's just that they're so *wild*. Mallory and I are absolutely in awe of her. I think Mary Anne is, too, a little. Claudia wears the newest, most up-to-date fashions (whatever they happen to be), and adds her own personal, slightly crazy touches. She loves art and sometimes makes herself jewelry, especially big earrings. (Claudia, of course, has pierced ears, which Mal and I want desperately but are not allowed to have yet. All we're going to get is braces on our teeth.)

Anyway, Claudia doesn't just love art, she's a really good artist. Unfortunately, she's a terrible student. Being a poor student is bad enough, but when you have an older sister who is a genius, like Claudia's sister, Janine, it's really tough. Claudia manages, though.

15

She does as well as she can in school, and otherwise concentrates on her art and baby-sitting. She lives with her parents, her sister, and her grandmother, Mimi.

Mary Anne Spier is the club secretary. She's in charge of keeping the record book in order, except for the money stuff. (That's Dawn Schafer's job, since she's the treasurer.) It's hard to believe that Mary Anne and Kristy are best friends. This is because in a lot of ways they're opposites. Oh, they look alike, all right. They're the two shortest kids in their grade and they both have brown hair and brown eyes, but that's where the similarities end. Kristy is loud and outgoing, Mary Anne is shy and introspective. (*Introspective* is one of my favorite words. It means thoughtful, looking inside yourself.) And Mary Anne is sensitive and caring. I notice that the other girls usually go to her if they have a problem. She's a good listener and takes people seriously.

Mary Anne, believe it or not, is the only club member with a steady boyfriend. She used to dress very babyishly, but now her clothes look pretty cool. She's changing. Claudia says she's becoming more mature. And I think that's hard on Kristy. Mary Anne lives with her dad and her kitten, Tigger. Her mother died when she was a baby. I think Mr. Spier used to be really strict with her, but he's lightened up lately.

Okay. Remember that I said there used to be a club member named Stacey McGill? She was the original treasurer of the Baby-sitters Club, but her family moved back to New York City, where they used to live. Guess what. *Our* family moved into her old house! Anyway, when Stacey moved away, Dawn Schafer took her place as the treasurer. Dawn had moved to Stoneybrook from California several months after Kristy started the club. She got to be good friends with Mary Anne, and soon she had joined the club. I like Dawn a lot. She lives near Mallory, so I see her more often than the other older girls in the club.

Dawn would be the first one to describe herself as a true California girl. She has long (and I mean *long*) hair that's so blonde it's almost white. She loves health food (won't touch the junk food that Claudia's addicted to) and always longs for warm weather.

She's going through a rough time right now. The reason she moved east was because her parents got divorced. She came here with her mom and her younger brother, Jeff. But Jeff was so unhappy that he finally moved *back* to California to try living with Mr. Schafer. As

Dawn pointed out, her family is now ripped in half. I think Dawn is a survivor, though.

The other club members are Mal and me. You already know about me. And you know that Mal has seven brothers and sisters. She loves to read, write stories, and illustrate her stories. She thinks her parents treat her like an infant, and she can't wait for the day when her braces will be off, her ears will be pierced, and her glasses will be gone. She's dying for contacts and wishes she could straighten out her head of curly hair. As Mal once said, being eleven is a real trial. Mal and I are junior club members since we are pretty much allowed to sit only after school and on weekends; hardly ever at night (unless we're at our own houses taking care of our brothers and sisters).

So those are our six club members. We do have two associate members, who don't come to meetings. They're people we can call on if we really get in a fix — if someone needs a sitter and none of us can take the job. One of those members is Logan Bruno, who just happens to be Mary Anne's boyfriend! The other is a girl named Shannon Kilbourne, who lives across the street from Kristy in her ritzy new neighborhood.

And that's about it. At our club meetings, we mostly take phone calls and line up jobs.

In between, we talk. We talk about us and what's going on in school or in our lives or with the kids we sit for. Sometimes we get silly. For instance, during the meeting that was held after my ballet tryouts, Dawn announced that she'd heard that if you were able to touch your nose with your tongue, it meant that eventually (like when you were eighteen) you would need a very big bra. Well, this was pretty intriguing for all of us, especially Mal and me, who don't need bras at all yet, and even though I didn't see the vaguest connection between tongue-touching and bra size.

"I can do it! I can do it!" Kristy shrieked, but she had to calm down in the middle of her shrieking because the phone rang. Kristy, who always sits in Claudia's director's chair, wearing a visor and looking official, dove for the phone. So did Mary Anne, Dawn, and Claudia. Mal and I didn't dive for it. We're too new for that. We're still in the middle of the fitting-in process.

Kristy picked up the phone and said, "Hello, Baby-sitters Club." She paused. "Yes? . . . Oh, I see. . . . Well, we've never sat for a deaf child before, but that doesn't make a difference to any of us. I mean, if it doesn't make a difference to you. We like all children." (Long pause.) "Training? Well, that makes sense. Listen, let me talk to the other baby-sitters and I'll call you back in a few minutes. Just give me your number. . . . Okay. Thanks. 'Bye."

Kristy hung up the phone and turned to us. "That was a new client. Her name is Mrs. Braddock. She's got two kids. Haley is nine and Matthew is seven. The Braddocks have just moved to the neighborhood. There are two hitches here. One, she needs a regular baby-sitter, two afternoons each week. And two, Matthew is deaf. He uses Ameslan, whatever that is. So she needs a sitter who can come every Monday and Wednesday afternoon, and she needs someone who'll be willing to learn this Ameslan thing. Mrs. Braddock says she'll train the sitter. She sounds really nice."

The six of us got into a big discussion. Dawn and Mary Anne didn't want regular afternoon jobs. They wanted their schedules to be more free. Claudia couldn't take the job because she has an art class on Wednesday. Kristy lives too far away to be convenient to the job. That left Mal and me. Mal was interested, but she often has to watch her brothers and sisters on Mondays when her mom volunteers at Meals on Wheels.

So Kristy called Mrs. Braddock back and I

got the job! I was so excited. Working with a handicapped child sounded really interesting.

The meeting was over then and we were all rushing out the door to our homes and our dinners when Mal cried, "Hey, Jessi, how did the tryouts go?"

"Oh, fine!" I replied lightly. "But I won't know anything until my next class."

"Well, good luck!" said the others.

"Thanks," I replied. But I was a whole lot more nervous than I let on.

CHAPTER 3

"And *one* and *two* and *three* and *four* and *plié . . . PLIÉ*, Mademoiselle Jones. Bend those knees!"

Sometimes Mme Noelle gets a little carried away in ballet class. She has this big stick (Becca saw it once and called it a club, but it really isn't) that she bangs on the floor in time to her counting. This is only when we're exercising at the *barre* at the beginning of class.

"And *one*" (bang) "and *two*" (bang) "and *three*" (bang) "and *four*" (bang). "On your toes. Up, up, *up!*"

I wished it were the end of class instead of the beginning. At the end, Mme Noelle was going to announce the parts in *Coppélia*. Not everyone from our class would wind up in the ballet. Kids in all the other classes at the school had tried out, too, and there were simply not enough parts to go around.

I looked at the students in the room. We are

an advanced *en pointe* class, which means that we dance in toe shoes. I will never forget how thrilled I was when I got my first pair of toe shoes. That is absolutely the most exciting thing in the life of a young ballerina. But you know what? We work out so hard that we need new shoes constantly. We just wear out one pair after another. Mama and Daddy admit that this is expensive, but they know I'm serious about my dancing, even if I don't want to become a professional, so they go along with it very nicely. I put quite a bit of my baby-sitting money toward shoes so that my parents don't have to pay for all of them.

In my class are eleven other girls. I'm the youngest and the newest. The next oldest are two twelve-year-olds, and the others are thirteen and fourteen. Mme Noelle said I'm the first eleven-year-old to be in this class in a long time. In fact, she sort of made an announcement about it. Right away I could tell that Hilary and Katie Beth were upset. Hilary and Katie Beth are the twelve-year-olds. Until I came along, *they* were the youngest in the class.

They do not like me.

Well, I'm sorry I took their special positions away, but I couldn't help it. I mean, I didn't do it on purpose.

"And *one* and *two* and *three* and — Pay attention, Mademoiselle Romsey!"

Mademoiselle Romsey. I mean, Ramsey. That's me! It always takes me a second to remember that.

In Mme Noelle's class, you don't apologize when she scolds you. You just shape up and work extra hard. Which I did.

But not until after I noticed Hilary and Katie Beth gloating at each other. They were happy to see me in trouble.

We finished our *barre* work and started in on some floor exercises. *Tour jetés* and stuff like that. We practiced head work, too. When you turn, you have to spin your head around faster than your body. It's sort of hard to explain. Anyway, then Madame began to teach us a complicated routine that involved groups of four girls dancing with their hands crossed and joined.

Nobody wanted to hold my hands.

Oh, okay. That's not true. It's just that Hilary and Katie Beth were in my group and neither of *them* wanted to hold my hands. The only solution was for me to dance at the end of the line, holding the hand of the fourteen-year-old in our group who was mature enough not to care about petty little things.

Mme Noelle finally ended class five minutes early.

"Okay, *mes petites*," she said, which is French for "my little girls." Considering the fourteen-year-olds in the class, *mes petites* seemed sort of odd, but she calls us that all the time.

She banged her club on the floor and said, "Gother 'round, please. I am going to announce those of you who have earned parts in *Coppélia*."

My heart began tap dancing in my chest. On the day of tryouts, all I had cared about was not doing something stupid. Since I hadn't done anything stupid, I was hoping that maybe, just *maybe*, I would be given a teeny little part, like one of the townspeople.

Mme Noelle cleared her throat as my classmates and I stood before her nervously. Most of us were nervous, anyway. But Hilary and Katie Beth looked smug. They thought of themselves as Madame's favorites, so I guess they weren't worried about getting good parts.

Madame began by announcing the smaller roles.

"In this closs," she said, "Mary Bramstedt and Lisa Jones will be two of the townspeople. Carrie Steinfeld will participate in the Donce of the Hours. Hilary, although the Chinese Doll is usually played by a male doncer, you have been given that part. I think you can do it. Katie Beth, you will play Coppélia herself."

Madame paused.

I nearly died. I wasn't even one of the *towns*people. How humiliating. And Hilary and Katie Beth were gloating up a storm. The Chinese Doll. What a role. And Coppélia herself. Oh, well. There probably weren't any black people in little European towns hundreds of years ago anyway. How could I have thought I'd get a role in *Coppélia*?

I was so busy feeling sorry for myself that I almost missed the next thing Madame said: "One role more. I am very pleased to announce that the part of Swanilda" (she's the star, remember?) "has been awarded to one of the students in this closs."

Just about everyone in the room gasped. I'm surprised there was any oxygen left to breathe.

"Swanilda," Mme Noelle said, "will be played by Mademoiselle Jessica Romsey."

Jessica Romsey? Oh, Jessica Ramsey. That was *me*. ME! *I* was going to be Swanilda, the star?

"I admit," Mme Noelle went on, "that Jessica is a bit young for the role, but I think she can hondle it. Jessica, your audition was wonderful. That is all. Soturday rehearsals will begin this weekend for those in the performance. Closs is dismissed."

I walked into the changing room in a fog. I wasn't sure how to feel. I was delighted, thrilled, scared to death. It was encouraging that Madame didn't seem to mind a black Swanilda, but could I really learn the part? I began to imagine myself on stage in Swanilda's lovely costume.

First I saw myself *pirouetting* and *tour jetéing* to beat the band.

Then I saw myself leaping through the air toward the open arms of Franz, missing, and sailing into the scenery, which comes crashing down, knocking three dancers unconscious, and ruining the performance.

With a little shudder I slipped off my shoes and leg warmers and searched around for my jeans.

"Congratulations, Jessi," said Mary Bramstedt and Lisa Jones.

I shook myself out of my fog.

"Thanks," I said, looking up gratefully. I smiled.

They crossed to the other side of the room and began sorting through their clothes.

"Congratulations, Jessi," said two more voices, only this time my smile faded. The voices were not friendly. They were nasally, mimicking what Mary and Lisa had just said. Imagine somebody noticing that you've totally botched something up, and saying, "Oh, that's *nice*. Real nice." That was exactly how those voices sounded.

I didn't have to glance up to see who the voices belonged to.

Hilary and Katie Beth.

What was I supposed to say?

I decided to ignore their tone. "Congratulations to you, too," I replied. "The Chinese Doll. That's a great part. And Coppélia, Katie Beth. That's terrific."

"Oh, come off it," replied Katie Beth nastily. She had unpinned her long hair and flipped it over her shoulder. "Coppélia barely does anything. She just sits there. She's a doll, for heaven's sake. They could put a dummy on stage, and it would be the same thing."

"No, it wouldn't," I told her.

Katie Beth just tossed her head. Then she took Hilary by the arm, and they sat down not far from me.

It was while I was pulling my shirt on over my leotard that I heard it.

"Teacher's pet," Hilary whispered to Katie.

They were talking about me.

"She just got the part because she's Madame's favorite. And she's the favorite because she's the newest and youngest," agreed Katie Beth.

"Yeah, just wait until another girl joins the class," Hilary added. "Then she'll see."

Were they right? Had I gotten the part of Swanilda because Madame favored new girls, not because I was a good dancer? If that were true, I couldn't stand it. That would be worse than not being in the production at all.

When I was dressed, I slunk out of school like a dog with its tail between its legs.

CHAPTER 4

I didn't worry about my role in *Coppélia* for long. In our house, it's hard to keep worries inside. Everyone notices when you're brooding. Even Squirt, who tries to make you laugh by blowing raspberries.

I hadn't been home from class for more than ten minutes before Mama dragged the whole story out. Then she began talking some sense into me. "Didn't we agree that the Stamford school was the best ballet academy in the area?" she asked me.

"Yes," I replied.

"And didn't we look into its reputation, and even the reputation of Madame Noelle?"

"Yes."

"And did we find anything that wasn't professional?"

"No."

"So," said Mama, who was really being a

30

lot gentler than this sounds, since she was sitting close to me on the couch and smoothing back my hair as she talked, "do you believe what those girls were saying? Do you think Madame Noelle would risk the whole show, would cast the starring role with a dancer who wasn't the best for the part, in order to play favorites?"

"Nope," I replied.

"I don't think so either," said Mama, and she pulled me close for a hug.

"Thanks, Mama," I whispered.

And that was the end of that. Hilary and Katie Beth were jealous, and I'd just have to live with that. It was their problem, not mine. The only way for me to feel bad about it was to *let* them make me feel bad. And I wasn't going to do that. Why should I?

I concentrated on Matthew Braddock, my new baby-sitting charge. I was supposed to go to his house for my first training session. I decided that before I did, I should at least know what Ameslan was. So the night before I met Matthew I went into our den and looked up some things in our encyclopedia. It turns out Ameslan is sign language and that signing is a way of talking with your hands — so that deaf people can *see* you talk, since they can't hear you. The book says signing is a lot easier than reading lips, because so many spoken words "look" the same. Stand in front of a mirror. Say "pad" and "bad." Do they look any different? Or try "dime" and "time." Do *they* look any different? Not a bit.

But signing is a language especially designed for the deaf, in which words or concepts are represented by different signs made with the hands. Actually, there are different kinds of sign languages, just like there are different spoken languages. American Sign Language (or Ameslan) was the language Matt had learned.

When I thought about it, even people who can hear use signs pretty often. We have always accused Daddy of "talking with his hands." He absolutely cannot hold them still when he talks. If he's talking about something big, he holds his hands wide apart. If he's trying to make a point, he pounds one hand on the table. If he wants to show that something is unimportant, he sort of waves one hand away. If he says your name, he points to you at the same time.

Well, I couldn't imagine a different sign for every word in the world, and I couldn't imagine the sign for a word like "shoe." Or how, for instance, would the sign for apple be different from the sign for orange?

I would find out soon enough.

I rang the Braddocks' bell at 3:15 on a Monday afternoon. I realized that from then on, my schedule was going to be very busy. Mondays — Braddocks, then a meeting of the Baby-sitters Club. Tuesdays — dance class. Wednesdays — same as Mondays. Thursdays — only free afternoon. Fridays — dance class, then club meeting.

Whew!

The door was answered by a pixie of a girl who must have been Haley, but who looked small for nine. Her blonde hair was cut short with a little tail in the back (*very* in), and her brown eyes were framed by luscious dark lashes. Her face was heart-shaped, and she gave me this wide, charming grin that showed a dimple at the right corner of her mouth.

"Hi," she said. "Are you Jessica?"

"Yup," I replied, "but call me Jessi. You must be Haley."

"Yup." (That grin again.) "Come on in."

Haley opened the door and I walked into a house that looked pretty much like Mallory's, only without all the kids. A lot of the houses in this neighborhood look the same. They were all built by this one guy, Mr. Geiger. I guess he didn't have much imagination.

As soon as I stepped inside, I was greeted by Mrs. Braddock. She looked like a nice, comfortable kind of mom to have. She was wearing blue jeans and Reeboks and a big, baggy sweater, and she rested one hand reassuringly on Haley's shoulder while shaking my hand with the other.

"Hi, Jessica — " she began.

"Jessi, Mommy," Haley interrupted. "Call her Jessi."

Mrs. Braddock and I laughed, and I was ushered into the living room. Then Mrs. Braddock told me to sit on the couch. "Matt hasn't come home from school yet, but he'll be here any minute. As you know, I'm not going out this afternoon. I mean, you're not here for official baby-sitting. I just want you to meet Matt and Haley, and I want to introduce you to sign language. If you're interested in learning it, we'll go on from there."

"Okay," I said. "Let's start. I love languages."

Mrs. Braddock smiled. "Terrific."

"Can I be the teacher, Mommy?" asked Haley.

"Does Haley know sign language, too?" I asked.

"We all do," replied Mrs. Braddock. "It's the only way to communicate with Matt, and we don't want him left out of anything." She turned to Haley. "You better be the assistant teacher, honey," she told her. "Why don't you start by finding the *American Sign Language Dictionary*? We'll lend it to Jessi for awhile."

Haley ran off and Mrs. Braddock continued. "Before I begin showing you actual signs, I should tell you a little about teaching the deaf, I guess. One thing you ought to know is that not everyone agrees that the deaf should communicate with sign language. Some people think they should be taught to speak and to read lips. However, in lots of cases, speaking is out of the question. Matt, for instance, is what we call profoundly deaf. That means he has almost total hearing loss. And he was born that way. We're not sure he's ever heard a sound in his life. He doesn't even wear hearing aids. They wouldn't do him any good. And since Matt can't hear any sounds, he can't hear spoken words, of course, and he can't imitate them either. So there's almost no hope for speech from Matt. Nothing that most people could understand anyway."

"And lip-reading is hard," I said. "I experimented in front of the mirror last night."

"You've been doing your homework," said Mrs. Braddock approvingly.

"How come everyone wants deaf people to speak and read lips?" I asked.

"Because if they could, they'd be able to communicate with so many more *hearing* people. Matt, for instance, can only communicate with us and with the teachers and students at his school. None of our friends knows sign language and only a few of our relatives do. When Matt grows older, he'll meet other deaf people who use sign language, and maybe even a few hearing people who can sign, but he'll be pretty limited. Imagine going to a movie theater and signing that you want two tickets. No one would know what you meant."

I could see her point and was about to ask why the Braddocks had chosen signing for Matt, when Mrs. Braddock continued. "We're not sure we've made the right choice, but that's the choice we made. At least we've been able to communicate with Matt for a long time now. Most kids take years to learn lip-reading and feel frustrated constantly, even at home." Mrs. Braddock sighed. "Some families," she added, "don't bother to learn to sign. The deaf children in those families must feel so lost."

Haley returned with a big book then and dropped it in my lap. "Here's the dictionary," she said cheerfully.

I opened it to the middle and looked at the pages in front of me. I was in the K section. The book reminded me of a picture dictionary that Becca used to have.

"Key" was the sixth word under K. I saw a picture of two hands — one held up, the other imitating turning a key in an imaginary lock on the upright hand.

"Oh, I get it!" I said. "This looks like fun."

"It is sort of fun," agreed Mrs. Braddock. "But there are several thousand signs in there."

"Several *thousand!*" I cried. I knew there were a lot of words in the world, but I hadn't thought there were *that* many.

"Don't worry," said Mrs. Braddock. She took the dictionary from me and closed it. "Right now, I'm just going to teach you a few of the signs that Matt uses the most. When you're at home you can use the dictionary to look up other things or things you forget, okay?"

"Okay," I replied, feeling relieved.

We were just about to start when the front

door opened and a little boy came into the living room. I caught sight of a van backing down the Braddocks' driveway.

"Well, there you are!" cried Mrs. Braddock, speaking with her voice and her hands at the same time. "Home from school."

The boy was Matt, of course, and his face broke into a grin just like Haley's, with a dimple on the right side of his mouth. He waved to his mother and then ran to her for a hug.

"Believe it or not," Mrs. Braddock said to me, "that wave was the sign for 'hello.' It's also the sign for 'good-bye.' "

"That's easy to remember," I said.

Mrs. Braddock turned Matt so that he could look at me. Then she turned him back to her and once again began signing and talking at the same time. She was introducing us.

"Is there a sign for my *name*?" I asked, amazed.

"That's a good question," Mrs. Braddock replied. "And the answer is 'Not exactly,' or perhaps, 'Not yet.' What I did just now was *spell* your name. I used finger spelling, which I'll explain later. However, since it takes too long to spell out names we use a lot, such as our own names, or the names of Matt's teacher and his friends at school, we make up signs for those people." Mrs. Braddock signed something to Matt, saying at the same time, "Matt, show Jessi the sign for your name."

Matt grinned. Then he held up one hand and sort of flew it through the air.

"That," said Mrs. Braddock, "is the letter M for Matt being tossed like a baseball. Matt loves sports."

"Oh!" I exclaimed. "Neat."

"Show Jessi the sign for Haley," Mrs. Braddock instructed Matt.

Another hand flew through the air.

"That was the letter H soaring like Halley's Comet. When you know finger spelling, you'll be able to tell the signs apart more easily. Also, we'll have to give you a sign soon."

Mrs. Braddock asked Haley to take Matt into the kitchen then and fix him a snack. When we were alone again, she began showing me signs.

"The word 'you' is easy," she told me. "Just point to the person you're talking to."

(What do you know? I thought. My father knows sign language!)

"To sign 'want,' " Mrs. Braddock went on, "hold your hands out like this — palms up, fingers relaxed — and pull them toward you, curling your fingers in slightly."

Mrs. Braddock went on and on. She showed me signs for foods, for parts of the body, and for the words "bathroom," "play," and "come." Finally she said, "I think that's enough for one day. I'm going to start dinner. Why don't you take Matt and Haley downstairs to the rec room so you can get to know them better?"

The Braddocks' rec room looked like any other rec room — a TV, a couple of couches, a shelf full of books, and plenty of toys.

"Ask Matt what he wants to play," I said to Haley.

Haley obediently signed to her brother, a questioning look on her face. Matt signed back.

"He wants to read," Haley told me.

"Read!" I cried. "He can read?"

"Well, he *is* seven," Haley pointed out, "and he's been in school since he was two. It's really important for him to be able to read and write."

Of course, I thought. Reading and writing are other ways to communicate.

Matt found a picture book and curled up with it.

"How can I get to know him if he reads?" I wondered out loud.

"How about getting to know *me?*" asked Haley impatiently, and she shot a brief look of annoyance at her brother. Luckily he didn't notice.

That one annoyed look said a lot. Something was going on between Matt and Haley, I thought, but I wasn't sure what.

That night I finished my homework and settled into bed with the *American Sign Language Dictionary*. Tons of questions came to me, and I wrote them down so that I'd remember to ask Mrs. Braddock. How do you sign a question? Do you make a question mark with your fingers? How do you make a word plural? I mean, if there's a sign for "apple," what's the sign for "apples"? What's finger spelling? (Mrs. Braddock had forgotten to explain.) And can you string signs into sentences, just like when you're speaking? (I wasn't sure, because I couldn't find signs for "the," or "an," or "a.")

Even though I knew I had a lot to learn, I decided I liked sign language. It's very expressive — almost like dancing.

CHAPTER 5

Wednesday

Brat, brat, brat.

Okay. We all agree that Jenny is spoiled and a little bratty, but I've never minded her too much. At least, not until today. Today she was at her worst. Mostly, she just didn't want to do anything. She wasn't dressed for anything fun and she wouldn't change into play clothes. Finally I took her outside and we ran into Jessi and the Braddocks! Then Jenny's brattiness just came pouring out. That kid needs a few lessons in manners. Really. Maybe we should start a class.

I have to admit that running into Mary Anne Spier and Jenny Prezzioso that afternoon was not the best experience of my life, but I guess it could have been worse. And it absolutely was not Mary Anne's fault. I bet Jenny was born a brat.

Oh, well. I'm ahead of myself (again). Mary Anne's afternoon at the Prezziosos' house began right after school ended. Mrs. P. let Mary Anne inside, where she found Jenny sitting at the dining room table having a snack. Now, come on. How many kids do *you* know who get afternoon snacks in the dining room? At our house, it's strictly kitchen. Usually we don't even sit down. Becca and I just open the fridge, stand in front of it until we see something we want, take it out, and eat it on the way to our rooms or (in my case) on the way to a baby-sitting job or to Stamford for dance class.

But Jenny was sitting at the dining room table eating pudding from a goblet with a silver spoon. She was wearing one of her famous lacy dresses. (Mary Anne once told me that she thinks the Prezziosos support the U.S. lace industry all by themselves.) On her feet were white patent leather Mary Janes, and in her hair were silky blue ribbons.

Now don't get me wrong. Jenny wasn't off to a birthday party or anything. Her mother dresses her like that every day. (I hope the time will come when Jenny will rebel and refuse to wear lace anymore. Or ruffles. Or ribbons. Or bows.) Another thing. The Prezziosos are not rich. They're just average. But Jenny is their princess, their only child. (They call her their angel.)

Anyway, Mrs. Prezzioso finally left, and Mary Anne and Jenny were on their own.

"Finish up your pudding, Jen, and then we can play some games," said Mary Anne brightly.

"I eat slowly," Jenny informed her. "And don't call me Jen."

(Keep in mind that Jenny is only four.)

"Sorry," Mary Anne apologized. But already her hackles were up, because she added tightly, "I didn't mean to insult you."

Jenny slurped away at her pudding. "All finished," she announced a minute later, holding out the spoon and goblet.

"Great," replied Mary Anne. "Go put them in the sink." She wasn't going to do Jenny's work for her.

Jenny did so, scowling all the way.

Mary Anne knew they were off to a bad start and began to feel guilty. "Okay!" she said.

"Let's play a game. How about Candy Land? Or Chutes and Ladders?"

Jenny put her hands on her hips. "I don't wanna."

"Then let's read. Where's *Squirrel Nutkin*? That's your favorite."

"No, it isn't, and I don't *wanna* read."

Jenny and Mary Anne were facing off in the kitchen, Jenny's hands on her hips.

"I know!" cried Mary Anne. "Finger painting!"

"Finger painting?" Jenny sounded awed. "Really?"

"Yes. . . . If you'll change into play clothes."

"No. No no no. This is my new dress and I'm wearing it."

"Okay, fine," replied Mary Anne. "If there's nothing you want to do then you can just stand here all afternoon. I'm going to read a book." (As you can probably imagine, quiet Mary Anne doesn't say things like that very often.)

Jenny looked at Mary Anne with wide eyes. "You mean you're not going to play with me?"

Mary Anne sighed. "What do you want to play?" she asked.

"I don't know."

"Dolls?"

"Nope."

"House?"

"Nope."

"You want to draw a nice picture for your mommy?"

"Nope."

Mary Anne had reached the end of her rope. "That does it," she muttered. She opened a closet door, pulled out Jenny's light coat (of course Jenny didn't own a sweat shirt or a windbreaker or anything), and put it on her. She buttoned it up, Jenny protesting the whole time, put on her own jacket, and marched Jenny outdoors.

"Now," said Mary Anne grimly, "we're going to have fun if it kills us."

But Jenny, if you remember, was wearing white patent leather shoes. They're kind of hard to have fun in. The only activity Mary Anne could think of for them was a nice quiet walk.

That was how they ran into Matt and Haley and me. I was at the Braddocks again and had just had another signing lesson. I had memorized over twenty signs by then. (The Braddocks knew about a million, but I was new at this. They'd been at it for years.) Anyway, after the lesson, Mrs. Braddock had asked me to take Matt and Haley outside to play.

Mary Anne and I were surprised to see each other.

"Hi!" we exclaimed.

Then we had to do a lot of introducing, since Jenny didn't know me or the Braddocks, Mary Anne didn't know the Braddocks, I didn't know Jenny, and the Braddocks didn't know Jenny or Mary Anne.

Haley translated for Matt, and I jumped in whenever I knew a sign. I noticed that Jenny was watching us with her mouth open.

"What are you doing?" she finally asked Haley and me.

"Matt's deaf," I explained. "He can't hear us, but we can tell him things with our hands. Then he can see what we're saying."

Jenny approached Matt and yelled right into his ear at the top of her lungs, "CAN'T YOU HEAR ME?"

Matt just blinked and backed up a few paces.

Haley signed to him to say hi to Jenny.

Matt obediently waved.

"He just said hi to you," I told Jenny.

"You mean he can't talk, either?" asked Jenny, aghast.

"He can make *sounds*," Haley told her defensively.

And just then, Matt caught sight of a bug wriggling along the sidewalk. He laughed. His laugh was a cross between fingernails on a blackboard and a goose honking. I had to admit, it was one weird sound.

Jenny cringed against Mary Anne. "Let's go," she whispered — loudly enough for Haley and me to hear her. "He's weird. I don't want to play with him."

"Well, you're not the first one to say so!" Haley shouted.

"We better leave," Mary Anne said quickly. "I'm sorry, Jessi. I'll call you tonight so we can talk, okay?"

I nodded.

As they left, Haley shot a murderous glance at her brother, who was now on his hands and knees, watching the bug.

"You know what?" she said to me, and her great grin was gone. "Having a brother like Matt really stinks." Then she stood behind him, tears glistening in her eyes, and shouted, "You stink, Matt! You STINK!" Of course, Matt didn't hear her.

"It is so horrible!" Haley went on. "People think Matt's weird, but he isn't. Deaf is not weird. Everybody's unfair." Then she stormed into the Braddocks' house and slammed the door behind her.

Ah-ha, I thought. I was beginning to understand Haley and Matt. The Braddocks had just moved to a new neighborhood and Haley wanted to fit in, but Matt was making that a little difficult.

Well, I could sympathize. In Stoneybrook, being black wasn't any easier.

CHAPTER 6

My first real baby-sitting job for Haley and Matt! I have to tell you that I was a little nervous. I was even more nervous than I'd felt at the most recent rehearsal of *Coppélia*. The rehearsal had been hard work and I'd felt sore afterward, but not nervous. I was fairly self-confident. So if I could dance the lead in a ballet, you'd think that a job baby-sitting for a nine-year-old and a seven-year-old one afternoon wouldn't be hard at all. And ordinarily it wouldn't be. But Matt is not your ordinary seven-year-old.

I still knew only a handful of signs, so I started imagining all sorts of problems. What if Haley wasn't around and Matt didn't feel well? I couldn't ask him what was wrong, and if he tried to tell me, I probably wouldn't understand.

But there was no point in worrying about things like that. Of course Haley would be there to help me, and Matt would be fine. Besides, he could write, and anyway, Mrs. Braddock was only going to the grocery store. She'd be gone for an hour and a half, tops.

When I got to the Braddocks' house I could tell that Mrs. Braddock was a little nervous, too. She kept reminding me about things.

"Be extra careful outdoors," she said. "Remember that Matt can't hear car horns."

"Right," I replied.

"And he can't hear a shouted warning."

"Right."

"And inside he can't hear the doorbell or telephone."

"I'll take care of those things."

"Do you remember the sign for 'bathroom'?"

"Yup."

"For 'eat'?"

"Yup. . . . And I can do finger spelling. I memorized the alphabet last night." (Mrs. Braddock had explained to me that there was a sign for every letter in the alphabet, just like there were signs for words. So, for instance, if I wanted to spell my name, I would sign the letters J-E-S-S-I. Finger spelling takes longer than regular signing, but at least you can communicate names and unusual words that way.)

"The whole alphabet?" Mrs. Braddock repeated. She sounded impressed.

I nodded. "The whole thing. Oh, and I thought of a name for myself. Look."

I shaped my right hand into the sign for the letter J (for my name), pointed it downward, and whisked it back and forth across the palm of my left hand. That's the sign for the word "dance" except that you usually make a V with your right index and middle fingers, to look like a pair of legs flying across the floor.

"See?" I said. "A dancing J! Anyway, don't worry, Mrs. Braddock. You know how many signs I've memorized. I'm not too good at sentences, but Matt and I will get along. No problem." I sounded a lot more confident than I felt.

"Besides," added Haley, who had appeared in the kitchen. "You've got *me*, right?" She sounded a little uncertain — as if I might say I didn't need her after all.

I put my arm around Haley. "I'll say!" I exclaimed. "You're the best help I've got."

Haley turned on that smile of hers.

"Well . . ." said Mrs. Braddock. She glanced down the hallway and out the front door, looking (I think) for Matt's special school bus. "Matt should be here in about ten minutes. I told him this morning that you would be here when he got home from school and that I'd be back soon. Haley can help you remind him if he seems anxious, but I think he'll be all right. He really likes you, Jessi."

"Thanks," I replied.

Mrs. Braddock left then, and Haley and I sat on the front stoop to wait for Matt. The school bus was prompt. It pulled into the driveway exactly ten minutes after Mrs. Braddock left.

Matt jumped down the steps of the van. He waved eagerly to the driver, who waved back, and then signed something to a giggling face that was pressed against a window of the van. The little boy signed back. A second boy joined in. Matt and his friends were talking about football. (I think.)

It was odd, I thought, to see so much energy and so much communication — without any sound at all. Watching the boys was like watching TV with the volume turned off.

The bus drove away and Matt ran across the lawn to Haley and me, smiling. (Mrs. Braddock hadn't needed to worry about anxiety.)

"Hi!" I signed to Matt. (A wave and a smile.)

He returned the wave and smile.

I showed him the sign for my name (which he liked), and then I asked him about school. (The sign for school is clapping hands — like a teacher trying to get the attention of her pupils. When I found that out, I wondered what the sign for "applause" or "clap" is, since it seemed to have been used up. This is the sign: You touch your hand to your mouth, which is part of the sign for "good," and *then* clap your hands. It's like applauding for good words. See why I like languages? They make so much sense.)

Matt signed back, "Great!" (He pointed to his chest with his thumb and wiggled his fingers back and forth — with a broad grin.)

After Matt had put his schoolbooks in his room, he ate a quick snack. I'll give you the sign for the snack. See if you can guess what the snack was. You form your hand into the sign for the letter A, then you pretend to eat your thumb. That's the sign for . . . apple! Eating the letter A. Isn't that great?

Anyway, as soon as Matt was finished eating, I took him and Haley outdoors. I had a plan. I hadn't been able to stop thinking about what happened when the Braddocks and I ran into Mary Anne and Jenny Prezzioso. And I was determined that Matt and Haley were going to make friends in their new neighborhood. I remembered how horrible Becca had felt when nobody in Stoneybrook would play with her. Then one day Charlotte Johanssen, who's just her age, had come over, and Becca was so happy she barely knew what to do.

I began marching Matt and Haley over to the Pikes' house.

"Where are we going?" Haley asked me.

"We," I replied, "are going to a house nearby where you will find eight kids."

"Is one of them my age?" Haley sounded both interested and skeptical.

"Yup," I replied and suddenly realized that we were leaving Matt out of the conversation by not signing. I told Haley to sign.

"I hope the nine-year-old isn't a boy," Haley said, hands flying.

(Matt made a face at that.)

"Nope," I said. "The nine-year-old is a girl. Her name is Vanessa. She likes to make up rhymes." There was no way I could sign all that, so Haley did it for me, to keep Matt informed. Then she told him where we were going.

"Is there a seven-year-old Pike?" Matt signed.

Haley looked at me.

I nodded. Then I signed "girl," and Matt made a horrible face. It wasn't a sign, but it could only mean one thing — YUCK!

"Tell him there's an eight-year-old boy," I said to Haley.

Matt brightened, and I finger spelled N-I-C-K-Y.

We had reached the Pikes' front door by then. Matt boldly rang the bell. It was answered by Mallory, and I was relieved. I'd told her we might come over, and I wanted her to help me with the introductions.

"The Barretts are here, too," she whispered, as we stepped inside. "They're friends from down the street. Buddy is eight and Suzi is five." She turned to Haley and Matt, said hello, and waved at the same time. She knew that much about signing from me. I loved her for remembering to do it. That's one of the reasons she's my new best friend.

"Well," said Mallory, "everyone's playing in the backyard."

We walked through the Pikes' house, waving to Mrs. Pike on the way, and stepped into the yard. It looked like a school playground.

The Pikes and the Barretts all stopped what they were doing and ran to us.

The introductions began.

The signing began.

The explaining began.

The staring began.

And Haley began to look angry again.

I glanced at Mallory. "Ick-en-spick," she whispered. And with that, a wonderful idea came to me. Mallory and I love to read, and not long ago we'd both read a really terrific book (even if it was a little old-fashioned) called *The Secret Language*, by Ursula Nordstrom. These two friends make up a secret language, and "ick-en-spick" is a word they use when something is silly or unnecessary.

"You know," I said to the kids, "maybe Matt can't hear or talk, but he knows a *secret language*. He can talk with his *hands*. He can say anything he wants and never make a sound."

"Really?" asked Margo (who's seven) in a hushed voice.

Mallory smiled at me knowingly. "Think how useful that would be," she said to her brothers and sisters, "if, like, Mom and Dad punished you and said, 'No talking for half an hour.' You could talk and they'd never know it."

"Yeah," said Nicky slowly. "Awesome."

"How do you do it?" asked Vanessa. "What's the secret language?"

This time, Haley jumped in with the answer. "It's this," she replied. She began demonstrating signs. The kids were fascinated.

"Say something," Claire, the youngest Pike, commanded Matt.

"He can't hear you," I reminded Claire.

"*I'll* tell him what you said," Haley told

Claire importantly. She signed to Matt.

Matt began waving his hands around so fast that all I could understand was that he was signing about football again.

Haley translated. "Matt says he thinks the Patriots are going to win the Super Bowl this year. He says — "

"No way!" spoke up Buddy Barrett. Haley didn't have to translate that. Matt could tell what Buddy meant by the way he was shaking his head.

Matt began signing furiously again.

"What's he saying? What's he saying?" the kids wanted to know.

Mallory and I grinned at each other. We sat down on the low wall by the Pikes' patio, relieved, and watched the kids.

"Your brothers and sisters are great," I said.

"When you grow up in a family as big as mine," Mallory replied, "you end up being pretty accepting."

"Thank goodness."

After awhile I looked at my watch and realized that Mrs. Braddock would probably be back from the grocery store soon.

"I better take Haley and Matt home," I said and began to round them up. But in the end, I only brought Matt home. Haley was having too much fun at the Pikes' to leave, and swore up and down that she knew the way back to her house. I left her teaching the kids how to sign the word "stupid." I had a feeling there was going to be a lot of silent name-calling in the neighborhood for awhile.

CHAPTER 7

Friday

Oh, no! Jessi what have you started? Mallory and I were sitting at her house last night and guess what happened! You won't believe it.

Well, she might believe it. Don't jump to any conclusions. After all, most kids like languages, and this one reminds my brothers of ~~football~~ signals.

Okay, so she'll believe it, but anyway, Jessi, get this. It started when the Pike kids went totally wild last ni

Not me! I wasn't wild!

No, of course not, Mal. You were one of the sitters. I meant that your brothers and sisters were wild.

Oh, okay.

I have to stop Dawn and Mal's notebook entry here. It goes on forever. Let me just tell you what happened while they were sitting. (And by the way, Dawn was right. I did sort of start something.)

Mr. and Mrs. Pike were going to a dinner party that evening, so Mallory and Dawn were in charge of the Pikes from six o'clock until eleven o'clock. They had to give the kids dinner and everything. I know you met some of the Pikes in the last chapter, but just to refresh your memory, I'll include all their names and ages here:

Mallory — the oldest, of course. She's eleven, like me.

Byron, Adam, and Jordan — ten-year-old triplets

Vanessa — nine

Nicky — eight

Margo — seven

Claire — five

Those kids are a handful, even for two experienced sitters.

When Dawn arrived, which was just as Mr. and Mrs. Pike were leaving, the kids were hungry and clamoring for dinner. Sometimes Mrs. Pike lets the kids eat up leftovers when baby-sitters are in charge, sometimes it's up to the sitters to make sandwiches or something. But this time Mrs. Pike had fixed a huge pot of spaghetti (a food that every single Pike will eat), and left the sauce bubbling away on the stove.

"Well, if everyone's hungry," said Mallory as her parents' car backed down the driveway, "then let's eat."

Dawn had sat at the Pikes often enough that she was prepared for what happened next: The kids swarmed through the kitchen and had the big table set and the food served in about thirty seconds. (Well, maybe I'm exaggerating, but it was fast.)

Then they sat down to their dinner. Since there are so many Pikes, their kitchen table looks like a table in the school cafeteria — very long with a bench on either side and a chair at each end. Four kids sit on one side, four on the other, and Mr. and Mrs. Pike sit in the chairs.

That night, the boys were lined up on one side, facing Vanessa, Claire, and Margo. Mallory was sitting where her mom usually sits and Dawn had taken Mr. Pike's chair. Something about boys *versus* girls seemed a little dangerous to Dawn, but there are almost no rules in the Pike house, so she didn't ask them to change places. She just hoped for the best.

That was before the worm song began.

Things started off innocently. Adam, one of the triplets, formed his spaghetti into a mound and placed a meatball at the very top. Then he began to sing (to the tune of "On Top of Old Smoky"), *"On top of spaghetti, all covered with cheese, I lost my poor meatball when somebody sneezed."*

Adam glanced at Jordan, who faked a very good sneeze.

"Ew, ew!" cried Claire. "Cut it out! Germs!"

The boys ignored her. Adam continued his song. *"It rolled off the table and onto the floor, and then my poor meatball rolled out the front door. It rolled down the sidewalk and under a bush, and now my poor meatball is nothing but mush."*

Adam looked as if he were going to send his meatball down the spaghetti mountain, and maybe, actually, out the front door, so Mallory leaned over and speared it with her fork.

"Hey!" exclaimed Adam. "Give it! That's mine!"

Meanwhile, Jordan, Byron, and Nicky were hysterical at the thought of a traveling meatball and were experimenting with theirs. They rolled meatballs down spaghetti mountains until Dawn told them that if they couldn't behave, she and Mallory would have to separate them.

"We'll behave," Adam spoke up from the other end of the table, "if Mallory will give me my meatball back."

Mallory returned the stolen meatball.

For two minutes, Dawn and the Pikes ate peacefully. The mounds of spaghetti and meatballs were disappearing.

Then, so quietly that Mallory and Dawn weren't sure at first that they'd heard anything, Nicky began singing the worm song. But he was eating at the same time, and he looked totally innocent.

"*Nobody likes me,*" he sang, "*everybody hates me. Guess I'll go eat worms.*" He picked a single strand of spaghetti off his plate and held it above his mouth.

"Nicky," warned Mallory.

Nicky dropped the spaghetti into his mouth. "*First one was slimy,*" he sang.

"Mallory, Dawn, make him stop!" cried Margo. "I'm going to be sick."

Margo is famous for her weak stomach. Everything makes her throw up — riding in the car, airplane takeoffs and landings, roller coasters. Those are motion sicknesses, of course, but Dawn thought there was a good chance that a gross-out would make Margo get sick, too. And she certainly didn't want anybody throwing up at the table, especially throwing up spaghetti.

But it was too late. Too late to stop the worm song, I mean.

By then, Byron was holding a strand of spaghetti over *his* mouth. "*Second one was grimy*," he sang, continuing the song.

"Mallory!" shrieked Margo, looking a little green.

"Oh, no! Oh, no! Not the worm song! Please stop the boys before something goes wrong," said Vanessa Pike, future poet.

Adam sucked in two strands of spaghetti, pretended to gag, and sang, "*Third and fourth came up.*"

At that point, Margo jumped up from the table and headed for the nearest bathroom.

Silence.

Margo stopped, turned around, looked at her brothers and sisters, and said, "Fooled you!"

She returned to the table. All the boys stuck their tongues out at her. Margo looked pleased with herself.

"That may have been a false alarm," said

Dawn, "but one more word of the worm song, and you will *all* be in trouble. Understand?"

"Yes," mumbled the Pikes.

They finished their dinner. It wasn't until they were clearing the table that the remainder of the worm song escaped from Nicky's mouth. It was as if he just couldn't help himself. He sang in a rush, "*So-I-began-to-crying-thinking-I-was-dying-eating-all-those-squishy-squashy-worms.*"

"That does it!" cried Mallory. "Didn't Dawn say no more worm song?"

The Pike kids scowled at Nicky.

"Yes," Nicky replied.

"I meant it, too," said Dawn. "You guys are banished to the rec room. I want you all down there for a half hour. No running, no jumping, no grossing each other out. Just *behave* for the next thirty minutes and let your sister and me finish cleaning up the kitchen."

Reluctantly, the seven Pikes headed down the steps to the rec room.

For ten minutes, Mal and Dawn worked in peace, scraping dishes, loading the dishwasher, and sponging off the table. They were almost done when they heard a giggle from the rec room. Then another and another.

But there were no crashes or shrieks or yelps.

"Maybe that means they've settled down," suggested Dawn hopefully.

The next thing my friends heard was Vanessa saying, "No, like this!"

"No, I've got it! Like *this!*" exclaimed Nicky. "Wiggle your fingers."

"How about an elephant?" said Margo. "That would be easy. You could make it look like you were flapping big ears."

"What would the sign for 'rabbit' be then?" wondered Byron. "They have big ears, too."

"No, they have *long* ones," Claire corrected him.

Upstairs in the kitchen, Dawn said to Mal, "What on earth are they doing?"

"Let's go see," she replied.

They tiptoed to the head of the stairs. In the rec room, the Pikes were seated on the floor in a sloppy circle, and their hands were working busily.

"Stupidhead!" Margo announced. She crossed her eyes and pointed to her head.

"Witch!" said Vanessa. She formed her hands into a peak over her head, making a witch's hat.

"Banana-brain," said Jordan. He touched his fingertips together, then separated his hands, indicating the shape of a banana. Then he tapped his head.

Mal and Dawn looked at each other in surprise.

"The secret language," whispered Mallory. "They're making up their own. I don't believe it."

"You're sure it's not the real thing?" said Dawn.

"You really think there's a sign in that dictionary of Jessi's for 'banana-brain'?"

"No," replied Dawn, giggling.

"We'll have to invite Haley and Matt over again," said Mallory carefully. "If my brothers and sisters like secret languages so much, then they ought to be able to learn the real thing."

"And if they did learn it," said Dawn slowly, catching on, "Matt could communicate with the kids in the neighborhood — with kids who can hear."

When Mallory told me this the next day, my heart leaped. It was more than I'd hoped for. It was like getting the part of Swanilda when I wasn't even sure I could be one of the townspeople.

The Pikes' secret language meant that they were going to accept Matt. I was sure of it. It meant that they wanted to communicate with him. I thought it might even mean that they would want to learn actual American Sign Language.

And it meant one more thing — that the kids would probably get to know and like Haley, just for herself.

I couldn't wait until Haley realized that.

CHAPTER 8

Rehearsal.

My bones ached. My muscles ached. Each and every one of my toes ached.

Being Swanilda was not easy.

It was four o'clock on a Saturday afternoon, and the cast of *Coppélia* had been rehearsing for hours.

"We want per-fec-see-yun," said Madame Noelle crisply. "Per-*fec*-see-yun." She banged her club on the floor. "Nothing less. Mademoiselle Parsons," (that was Katie Beth), "you must turn the head faster and start the turn a little later. Just a froction of a second, *non?* Mademoiselle Bramstedt," (that was Mary, one of the townspeople), "higher on the toes. This is a toe-doncing, *en pointe* production. Please to remember. Mademoiselle Romsey, excellent work."

I closed my eyes with relief. Thank goodness. That was all she'd said to me that day.

Of course, I'd been working extra hard — practicing longer hours at home and putting every ounce of *me* into my dancing.

The other cast members glanced at me approvingly. I was glad. I needed their approval. I wanted to show them that I could be a good Swanilda even if I was young and new at the school.

"Okay, closs. Our time is ended," said Madame. "This was a good rehearsal. Go change now. I will see you in your closses next week."

As I walked toward the dressing room, a hand touched my shoulder. I looked around. It was Katie Beth. She was with Hilary.

"Good work," said Katie Beth briskly.

"Yeah, good work," agreed Hilary. "Nice job."

They linked arms and walked away.

Not exactly friendly, but a whole lot better than the sarcastic comments they used to make. Katie Beth had almost smiled.

In the changing room, I got dressed slowly. Daddy had said he'd be a little late picking me up. Even though it was Saturday, he was in his office in Stamford. He was working on a special project and had a big deadline coming up. That morning he'd told me that he'd pick me up at 4:30, after some important meeting.

Although I changed my clothes slowly, I

was dressed by 4:10. I walked into the lobby of the school to wait for my father. I sat on a bench and watched the other students stream past me, out the front door. When things quieted down, I noticed Katie Beth sitting on another bench, not far away.

We smiled embarrassed smiles and looked at our hands.

After a moment, I looked up again. Katie Beth wasn't alone. Sitting next to her was a younger girl, about Haley's age. She looked somewhat like Katie, or would have if she'd pulled her long hair back from her face, the way Katie's was fixed.

Were they sisters? If they were, why weren't they talking? When Becca and I are together, we never shut up.

Katie Beth caught me looking at her and said, "This is my sister, Adele."

"Hi, Adele," I said.

Adele didn't answer, but when Katie Beth nudged her, she smiled at me.

I decided to take a big risk. I got up and moved to the bench next to Katie Beth and Adele. "I'm waiting for my father," I told them. "He won't be here until four-thirty." I checked my watch. "Fifteen more minutes."

Katie Beth nodded. "We're waiting for our mom. She's talking to Madame Noelle. She's

72

upset because I need new toe shoes so often."

I nodded understandingly. "My parents don't like it, either. But there's really nothing you can do about it."

"That's what I tried to tell Mom, but . . ."

Katie's voice trailed off and I knew she meant, "Go try to figure out parents."

I smiled.

Just then, Adele touched her sister on the arm. Katie Beth turned to look at her. To my great surprise, Adele signed "bathroom." She was using American Sign Language!

To my even greater surprise, Katie Beth looked at her sister as if she were a cockroach, and then turned back to me. She was blushing bright red.

Adele nudged Katie Beth again and signed "bathroom" for the second time. She was getting that look on her face that Becca sometimes gets which means, "This is an extreme emergency. I need the bathroom *now.*"

"Hey, Katie," I said, "Adele can use the bathroom down the hall. No one would mind." I signed that to Adele, who gave me the most incredibly grateful look you can imagine, jumped to her feet, and ran down the hall. As she passed me, hair flying, I caught sight of the hearing aids in her ears.

Katie Beth glanced at me, puzzled.

"She had to go to the bathroom," I told her.

"You mean you understood her?"

"Yes," I replied. "Didn't you?" I was sure "bathroom" was one of the most popular signs in sign language. It was probably the first one ever made up.

"No," Katie Beth answered in surprise. "I don't know sign language."

"You *don't?* But how do you live with Adele? How do you know wh — "

"Oh, I don't live with her," Katie Beth broke in. "Not really. She goes to a special school for the deaf. It's in Massachusetts. She lives there most of the time. She only comes home for holidays, part of the summer, and a few weekends."

"But when she's home," I pressed, "how do you talk with her?"

"Well, I don't exactly. I mean, my parents and I don't. Sometimes if we shout really loudly, she can hear us a little. And she can read lips, sort of."

"Does she talk?"

Katie Beth shook her head. "Nope. She could but she won't. She is so stubborn."

I wondered about that, considering the sounds I'd heard coming from Matt's throat.

Then another thought occurred to me Boy, was Matt ever lucky. How terrible it must be for Adele. She couldn't even communicate with her own family, unless they wrote everything down all the time, and I didn't think there was much chance of that.

I still wasn't sure that the Braddocks had done the right thing by teaching Matt only sign language, but I did see that they were a pretty incredible family. They'd kept him at home (Adele must have felt pushed off the face of the earth), and they'd *all* made the effort to learn and use sign language — fluently.

"You know," I said to Katie Beth, "sign language is fun. And in a way, it's like dancing."

"What do you mean?"

"Well, it's a way of expressing yourself using your body."

Katie Beth looked thoughtful. Then she asked, "How come you know how to sign?"

I told her about Matt. "I could show you some signs," I said as Adele returned from the bathroom.

"I don't know . . ."

"Oh, come on. It's fun. Look — this is the sign for 'dance.' " I demonstrated.

"Hey, cool!" exclaimed Katie Beth.

Adele was watching us. She smiled. Then she used her hands to ask me if I was a dancer like her sister.

I nodded. Then I asked her how old she was.

Adele held up one hand and formed her index finger and thumb into a circle, her other fingers pointing upward.

Nine. (There are signs for numbers, just like there are for letters.)

So she *was* Haley's age.

"Do you dance?" I signed to Adele.

She shrugged. Then she signed back that she couldn't hear the music, and she didn't know ballet, but she liked to dance in her own way.

During our signed conversation, Katie Beth had been watching us curiously. I knew she didn't know what Adele and I were saying to each other, and I wondered how she felt being left out of a conversation. At the Parsonses' house, Adele must always be left out.

"What are you saying?" Katie Beth couldn't resist asking.

I told her. Then I showed her the signs for a few more words. Adele was grinning away.

By the time Adele and Katie Beth's mother showed up, it was almost 4:30. I walked outside with the Parsonses to watch for Daddy's car.

"Good-bye!" called Katie Beth as they drove off. "And thanks! See you on Monday!"

" 'Bye!" I called back. Adele and I waved to each other.

I felt that something important had happened between Katie Beth and me. We were linked. She would never call me a teacher's pet again. But we probably also would not wind up as best friends. My only best friends were Keisha and Mallory. I was linked to them, too, but those links were much, much stronger.

CHAPTER 9

saturday

Jessie youre secret langage is a hit. Its catching on everywhere and its the best babysiting game ever invinted. I used it to ix exh entirtane karen andrew and David micheal.

See I sat at kristys house last night. tristy was at a baketball game with her big borthers Sam and Charlie. I love siting but the house scars me. And karen doesnt help with her gost stories and which stories. So last night when karen started with the ghost stuff I decided to show the kids a litle of the secret langage. They love it!

The secret language sure was catching on, and I couldn't have been happier. The more kids who learned it, even just a few words of it, the more kids Matt could "talk" to. I was really happy about Claudia's notebook entry. Of course, I knew before I read the entry that Claudia was teaching the secret language to Kristy's little brother, stepbrother, and stepsister. That was because Claudia and Karen kept calling me and asking me to look up things in the sign language dictionary. But, as usual, I'm getting ahead of myself. Let me start back at the beginning of the evening when Claudia arrived at Kristy's house.

Claudia's mother dropped her off at the Brewer mansion at seven o'clock. Claudia rang the bell, and it was answered by Karen Brewer, Kristy's stepsister. Kristy loves her stepbrother and stepsister just as much as if they were her real brother and sister. She wishes she could see them more often. But Karen and Andrew mostly live with their mother and stepfather. They only stay at their father's house every other weekend, every other holiday, and for two weeks during the summer.

Karen is this bouncy, bold little girl who loves to scare people (including herself) with stories about witches and ghosts. She's even convinced that her father's next-door neighbor, Mrs. Porter, is actually a witch named Morbidda Destiny. And she's sure that a ghost named Ben Brewer (some old ancestor of hers, I guess) haunts the third floor of her father's house.

Andrew, on the other hand, is shy and quiet. Karen often scares him, although she doesn't mean to. Usually, she's very protective of him, and he adores her.

That night, Claudia was going to be sitting for Karen, Andrew, and David Michael, Kristy's seven-year-old brother. Claudia arrived just as Kristy, Sam, and Charlie were running out the door to the Stoneybrook High *versus* Mercer High basketball game.

" 'Bye, Kristy! Hi, Karen!" said Claudia.

" 'Bye!" called Kristy as the door slammed behind her.

"Hi," said Karen. "I'm going to be very busy tonight. There's a ghost party on the third floor."

"And you're going to it?" asked Claudia, trying to look serious.

"Are you kidding?" replied Karen. "That would be crazy. But I'm in charge of refreshments. All night it's going to be my job to take food to the bottom of the third-floor stairs and leave it there for the ghosts."

"What are you going to feed them?"

"Ghost pâté," replied Karen. "It's really the only thing for a ghost party."

"Well, I'm sure they'll appreciate it," said Claudia.

"Hi, Claudia," spoke up another voice. It was Kristy's mother, the new Mrs. Brewer. "Thanks for coming. Mr. Brewer and I will be home by ten-thirty. And the kids should go to bed at nine."

"Aw, *Elizabeth*," complained Karen. "Andrew's younger than me. He should go to bed before I do."

"But it's Friday, honey," Mrs. Brewer pointed out. "He can stay up a little later."

"Then *I* get to stay up even later than he does."

Kristy's mother sighed. "All right. Claudia, Andrew's bedtime is nine o'clock, Karen's is nine-fifteen, and David Michael's is nine-thirty."

"Goody!" cried Karen, jumping up and down. "Thank you!" Claudia thought Karen might complain about David Michael's bedtime, but she didn't. Fair was fair.

"Now," Mrs. Brewer went on, "Andrew is

getting over tonsillitis and needs a spoonful of liquid penicillin before he goes to bed. The bottle is in the kitchen, in the cabinet next to the refrigerator."

"Okay," Claudia replied.

"I guess that's it. You know where the emergency numbers are. And Mr. Brewer and I will just be across the street at the Papadakises'."

The Brewers left, and Karen and Claudia went upstairs to the big playroom, where they found Andrew and David Michael building a space station out of Legos and Tinker Toys.

"Hi, guys," Claudia greeted the boys.

"Hi!" they replied.

"Want to help us?" asked Andrew.

"Sure." Claudia sat down in front of the space station.

"Well," said Karen, "I guess I better go."

"Go where?" asked Claudia vaguely, sifting through a pile of Legos.

"Down to the kitchen, then up to the ghosts."

"Down to the kitchen?" Claudia repeated. "For real food?"

"Sure. That's where the ghost pâté is."

"What's ghost pâté?" asked Andrew nervously.

"Don't worry about it," David Michael told him. "Karen's just pretending again."

"Am not!" cried Karen.

"Are too!"

"Hold it! Hold it!" said Claudia. (Silence.) "Karen, use pretend food, okay? You don't need to go down to the kitchen."

There were, Claudia thought, a few problems with living in a house as big as the Brewers'. For instance, it was easy for the kids to get out of earshot in the house, and Claudia didn't like that. And when she sat downstairs at night waiting for the Brewers to come home, she sometimes felt terrified.

Then Claudia added, "And Andrew, don't worry. It really is just a game."

"Is not!" said Karen indignantly. She stooped down, pretended to pick something up, and walked out of the room calling, "Here comes the pâté!"

When she returned, Claudia decided that it might be a good idea to get Karen's mind off the ghost party. First she tried to interest her in the boys' space station. When that didn't work, she said in a hushed, excited-sounding voice, "How would you guys like to learn a secret language?"

"Huh?" replied Andrew and David Michael. They didn't look up from their work.

But Karen said, "A secret language? What do you mean?"

"I," Claudia began, "can show you how to talk without making any sounds at all. Without even opening your mouth."

Now she had captured even the boys' attention. "That's impossible," said David Michael.

"No, it isn't." Claudia made the sign for "dance," which I had shown the members of the Baby-sitters Club. "That means 'dance,' " she informed them.

She showed them three other signs. "Some deaf people," she told the kids, "know thousands of signs. They can have whole conversations with their hands."

"Is there a sign for 'ghost'?" asked Karen.

"Probably," Claudia replied. "But I don't know what it is."

"Oh." Karen looked disappointed.

"I know how we can find out, though," Claudia said, brightening. "We'll call Jessi Ramsey. She has a dictionary with all the signs in it. She can look up 'ghost.' "

The four of them trooped into the hallway, and Claudia dialed my number. Becca answered the phone and called me into our kitchen. When Claudia had explained what was going on, I said, "Just a sec. I'll go get the book."

I ran to my room, grabbed the dictionary off my desk, and tried to look up "ghost" as I was running back to the kitchen. "Here it is!" I exclaimed. (I was pleased to be able to help Claudia. Sometimes Mal and I feel like the babies of the Baby-sitters Club, since we're younger and have been members for such a short time.) "There *is* a sign for ghost. Only it's going to be kind of hard to describe."

I did my best.

Then Karen wanted the sign for "witch." That one was almost impossible to explain over the phone. After "witch," she wanted "cat," "storm," "night," and "black."

I thought that was the end of things, but no sooner had I put the dictionary away than the phone rang again. This time it was Karen herself.

"I forgot the sign for 'night,' " she said.

I tried to explain it again.

"And is there a sign for 'afraid'?"

"What are you going to do?" I asked Karen. "Sign a ghost story?"

"Yes," she replied seriously.

I smiled. "Okay." (The sign for "afraid" is covering your heart in fear with both hands. I love it, I just love it.)

Meanwhile, back at Kristy's house, Karen

was trying to sign her ghost story. She didn't know nearly enough words, though, and soon gave up.

"Let's make ourselves a snack and then you guys will have to start getting ready for bed," Claudia told the kids.

"What kind of snack?" asked Karen.

"Whatever you want," Claudia replied. "But if you have the right ingredients, I'll fix *you* ghost pâté."

Luckily, Claudia found what she needed — crackers and liverwurst. She spread a saltine with liverwurst and handed it to Karen. "There you go," she said. "Ghost pâté."

"Yick," said Andrew.

But Karen ate her snack eagerly. "*Thank* you, Claudia," she said several times, glad that someone was taking her game seriously.

When the snacks were eaten and the kitchen was clean, Claudia gave Andrew his medicine, and then took the kids back upstairs. "Time to get ready for bed now," she said. "Andrew, you first."

While she was giving Andrew a hand, she thought she heard Karen on the phone in the hall, but she didn't think anything of it. Andrew's room was a mess and he couldn't find his pajamas. Then he got worried about the ghost party again.

"Honest. It's not real," Claudia told him. "Karen made it all up."

"Then why did you make the ghost pâté?" he asked.

Oops.

"That was just silly," said Claudia. "It was pretend."

Andrew found his pajamas, put them on, and went into the bathroom to brush his teeth. When he returned, he climbed into bed.

"I won't be able to fall asleep," he announced. "I'm scared."

"Sure you will," Claudia told him. "You'll fall asleep. Count something, like sheep."

"I'll have to count ghosts," Andrew said.

"Well, at least count friendly ones. There *are* friendly ghosts, you know."

"There are?"

"Yup."

"How do you tell them from the spooky ones?"

"The friendly ones are the ones who smile and call, 'Hi, Andrew!' The spooky ones just say, 'BOO!' "

"Oh."

"Call me if you need me."

"Okay. Night, Claudia."

"Night, Andrew."

Click. Light off.

Creak. Door open a crack.

Claudia tiptoed down the hall to Karen's room, where she found her sitting on her bed holding Tickly, her blanket, in one hand, and Moosie, her stuffed cat, in the other.

"We have time for a story, don't we, Claudia?" she said. "We have until nine-fifteen. Fifteen more minutes."

"Right," replied Claudia. "What do you want to hear?" And then she went on in a rush, "How about *The Cat in the Hat?*" She suggested that because Karen always suggests *The Witch Next Door* or one of her other witch stories, and Claudia had had enough ghost and witch tales for one night.

"Okay," agreed Karen.

So they read the book, lying side by side on Karen's bed.

When they were finished, Claudia returned the book to its shelf while Karen snuggled under the covers next to Moosie and Tickly.

"Good-night," said Claudia.

Karen didn't say anything, but she pulled her arms out from under the covers. She signed something to Claudia.

"What was that?" asked Claudia.

"It was 'good-night'! I called Jessi again while you were helping Andrew get ready for bed."

Claudia signed "good-night" back to Karen.

Then Karen made another sign. "I love you," she said.

Claudia smiled and signed back. She switched on Karen's nightlight and quietly left the room, remembering to crack her door open like Andrew's.

Then she tiptoed down the hall to David Michael's room, thinking that signing was the nicest language she had ever seen.

CHAPTER 10

I was baby-sitting regularly at the Braddocks' now. I loved it, but my schedule was tough. On Tuesday and Friday I went to my dance class and sometimes stayed later than usual, trying to keep in shape for rehearsals. Rehearsals were held on the weekends, and often on Thursday as well, which *had* been my only free afternoon of the week. But every Monday and Wednesday afternoon I went directly from school to Matt and Haley's house. Then Mrs. Braddock would leave for her part-time job. She was working with deaf adults at the Stoneybrook Community Center.

The Braddocks and I had a routine. I would reach their house at three o'clock, just a few minutes after Haley got home from Stoneybrook Elementary. Then Mrs. Braddock would leave and I would fix a snack for Haley and me. After we'd eaten, we'd sit on the front stoop and wait for Matt's bus to drop him off.

Then *Matt* would eat a snack, and when *he* was finished we'd go outside to play. We'd play with the Pikes, the Barretts, and sometimes even Jenny Prezzioso, who seemed to accept Matt a little more than she had the first time she'd met him. On rainy days we had to stay in, of course, but we invited kids over, or went to somebody else's house. We were always with other kids, and Matt and Haley were eating it up.

Plus, the secret language was spreading fast. Learning signs was a game, and the kids, especially Vanessa and Nicky Pike, learned them quickly. This was great, because Vanessa and Haley were getting to be friends, and Nicky, Matt, and Buddy Barrett were getting to be friends, too. They often needed Haley (or me) to translate for them, but the friendship was growing anyway.

One day, the weather was warmer than usual.

"Summer!" Matt signed to me excitedly. He crooked his right index finger and imitated somebody wiping a hot forehead.

I smiled at him. It wasn't summer, though, so I signed, "It *feels* like summer."

Matt nodded. He had just finished his snack and we were heading outside to play. We opened the front door and found the Pike triplets, Buddy Barrett, and Nicky crossing the Braddocks' lawn.

"Hi!" Matt waved eagerly.

The boys waved back.

"Where's Vanessa?" Haley called.

"She had to go to the dentist," Nicky answered.

"Oh." Haley sounded disappointed.

The boys began a game of six-person baseball. They didn't need to talk much to play that.

Haley and I sat down on the steps and watched them.

Buddy hit the ball out into the street, ran the bases, and jumped up and down as if he'd scored a home run.

"No fair!" Nicky shouted angrily.

"The ball was out!" Matt added.

I was about to remind the boys to sign when suddenly they remembered on their own. Nicky signed, "No fair!", Matt signed "The ball was out," and then Jordan jumped in.

"No!" he signed. "Safe."

Haley and I looked at each other.

"They're not bothering to talk at *all*," said Haley, awed.

"Nope," I replied. "They've learned every sign that could possibly have anything to do with football or baseball."

Haley grinned. "It's a good thing Matt plays sports so well. If he didn't, I don't know what I'd do."

"What do you mean?" I asked.

"Well, it's sure helped him make friends here."

"I know," I said, "and that's great. But what does that have to do with you? You said if *he* wasn't good at sports, you didn't know what *you'd* do."

"I have to help him," Haley said simply. "I have to watch out for him."

"You do? I'm the baby-sitter," I teased.

Haley smiled. Then her smile faded and she looked sort of sad. "You're not Matt's sister," she told me.

"No, I'm not."

"You don't know what it's like."

"That's true. . . . What *is* it like?"

"You have to stand up for him when kids tease him. But while you're doing it, you wish you weren't."

"How come?"

"Because it makes you as weird as Matt. And that makes you hate Matt sometimes." Haley paused and corrected herself. "Well, not hate him. But . . . oh, what's the word?"

"Resent?" I suggested. "You resent Matt?"

"Yeah." Haley looked ashamed.

"Don't feel bad about it," I said. "I resent my brother and sister sometimes, too. Like when Mama asks me to give Squirt a bath or something and I want to practice my ballet."

Haley nodded. "But your brother and sister aren't deaf."

"So? Why should you have to be a perfect person just because your brother *is* deaf?" I asked Haley. "That doesn't make any sense to me. Matt's not special, he's just different."

"He is too special!" cried Haley.

I smiled. "I'm glad you think so. What I meant was that basically, Matt's like most other seven-year-old boys. Except that he's deaf and you have to use sign language to talk to him. But look. Look at Matt right now."

Matt, Nicky, and Adam were jumping up and down because their team had earned another run. Matt stuck his fist in the air like a proud athlete. Nicky and Adam imitated him.

Haley couldn't help grinning. "I really love him," she said. "And I'm proud of him. He's smart, he works hard, and even though he's different, he tries to make himself as *not* different as possible. And he's only seven! But, boy, sometimes I wish . . . I know this is really, really awful, Jessi, but I guess I can tell you. I've never told anyone else, though."

"What?" I asked her.

"Sometimes I wish he'd never been born."

I was a little surprised at what Haley had said, but when I thought about it, it made sense. I tried to be matter-of-fact. After all, her feelings were her feelings. They didn't make her a bad or a good person. Still, she had surprised me.

"Well," I said slowly, "I can understand that. I really can. I've wished the same thing sometimes about Becca and Squirt. More with Becca, maybe, since she's so close to my age. But I've felt it with Squirt, too. Sometimes I think, boy, wouldn't it be great to be an only child. I'd have Mom and Dad all to myself, and no one would ever interrupt me while I was practicing or trying to do my homework, and no one would ever snoop in my room or take my things without asking. But then I think, if I didn't have Becca, who could I giggle with late at night? And who could I complain to? Sometimes the kids at school tease me because I'm black, and *no one* knows how that feels the way Becca does."

Haley nodded thoughtfully. "I guess you do understand," she told me. (She sounded very grateful.) "You know, all I really want is a family who talks with their mouths, not their hands. A little brother who doesn't make wild-animal noises, who walks to Stoneybrook Elementary instead of riding that dumb van to Stamford everyday."

"Who doesn't embarrass you," I added.

"Right. And then sometimes . . . sometimes I don't know what I'd do without him. Look at this." Haley reached under her blouse and pulled out a gold chain. Hanging from it was a wobbly-looking round pendant painted red with an H scratched in it. You could tell the pendant had been made from clay. "Matt made this for me in art class," she said. "He gave it to me for Christmas last year. I always wear it. This is really weird but, like, I'll be totally mad at Matt for embarrassing me or something, and then I'll remember the necklace and I can't feel mad at him at all. I'll just want to, you know, protect him and stuff."

I did know. "Yup," I said. "Once I was mad because Becca got sick and Mama made me miss a ballet class to watch Squirt while she took care of Becca. I wanted to kill Becca . . . and Squirt. Then Squirt put his arms around me and said, 'Dur-bliss?' and I started laughing and wasn't mad at all."

Haley giggled. We stopped talking for awhile. I felt like I was finally beginning to understand the Braddock kids.

We watched Matt hit a home run and that was when Haley said to me, "You know, if

Matt had to be handicapped, I'm glad he was made deaf. If he was crippled or blind he probably wouldn't be playing baseball right now. I think he'd be able to do a lot less. Being deaf, well, maybe he can't talk well or hear, but think what he *can* do. Almost anything. He can even watch TV. With closed-captioned TV you get this special decoder, and then you can *read* some shows: The words the people are saying are written on the screen. It's like watching a movie with subtitles. So really the only thing Matt can't do is go to a concert or a play or something."

I'd been thinking about something I'd read recently. Someone, Helen Keller, I think, had noted that blindness only separates you from *things*, while deafness separates you from *people*. So I was about to disagree with Haley, but what she had just said caught my attention.

"Matt's never been in a theater?" I asked. "He's never been to any kind of performance?" How awful.

"Well, sometimes his school puts on plays in sign language," said Haley.

"But imagine," I murmured. "Never been to a ballet or a musical . . ."

"Well, he couldn't hear the music," Haley pointed out.

"I know," I replied, remembering my conversation with Adele. I was also remembering Mme Noelle's club. I was thinking about when we do warm-ups and Madame roams around the ballet studio saying, "And *one* and *two* and *three* and *four*," banging that club. When she walks by you, you can feel the vibrations of the club hitting the floor. You can also feel the vibrations of the piano music Madame's assistant sometimes plays. If you stand with your hands resting on top of the piano you can feel soft and strong hums.

I thought about *Coppélia*. I thought about how much more there was to a ballet than the music. There was plenty to see — the dancing and the costumes and the scenery. Plus, it was just plain exciting to be in a theater — to look at the rows and rows of red seats and watch the ushers showing people up and down the aisles and hold your breath when the lights go down and the curtain goes up.

I was getting an idea. It was a really terrific idea, but I didn't say anything about it to Haley then, just in case I couldn't pull it off.

Still, as soon as I got home that evening, I began working on the idea. I decided that the first thing to do was to have a talk with Mme Noelle.

CHAPTER 11

My plan was working! It really was. I was very excited. I'd spoken to Mme Noelle, to Mrs. Braddock, and even to the head of my whole dance school. Nothing was settled, but everything was "in the works" (as Daddy would say).

One Friday, I got to Claudia's house for a club meeting a couple of minutes after five-thirty. I charged up the Kishis' walk, skidded to a stop, rang their bell, heard Claudia yell, "Come in!" and charged up to her room. As usual, I was the last to arrive. I hadn't even had time to change completely after ballet class, so I was wearing my leotard and a pair of jeans. My hair was still pulled back tightly, the way Madame says we must wear the hair during closs.

"Hi," I said when I entered the headquarters of the Baby-sitters Club. Even though I was only two minutes late and everyone knew I had a tight schedule because of dance class, I felt a little nervous. After all, Kristy could be sort of strict. Besides, Mal and I, as the newest and youngest club members, felt that we better not make any mistakes. We didn't want to stir up trouble, and we felt we had to prove ourselves.

"Sorry I'm late," I apologized.

I checked out Claudia's room. People were in their usual places: Kristy was in the director's chair, Mary Anne, Dawn, and Claudia were sitting on the bed, and Mal was on the floor. She and I always end up down there. The room was a cluttered mess, but I could see that Mal had cleared a space for me next to her.

Claudia's room is always a mess — for two reasons. 1. She's a pack rat. She's a really good artist and likes to keep all kinds of stuff on hand — bottle caps, interesting pebbles, scraps of fabric, bits of this and bits of that, not to mention her paper and canvases and paints. She never knows what she might need for a sculpture or a collage. 2. Claudia is also a junk-food addict. She likes Ho-Ho's, Yodels, pretzels, candy, gum, etc., but her parents don't approve of this habit, so Claudia has to hide the stuff around her room. Then sometimes she forgets where she's hidden it and has to go rooting through all her stuff to find it.

Anyway, Kristy accepted my apology with no problems.

I plopped down next to Mal.

"Ring-Ding?" asked Claudia, holding one out to me.

I smiled, but shook my head. "No thanks."

"Double-Stuff Oreo?" she tried again.

"I better not. I'd love one, but I think I'll wait for dinner." I like junk food as much as Claudia does, but I try not to eat too much of it. Ballerinas have to be strong and agile and in good shape. Junk food doesn't help you to be any of those things.

"Okay, said Kristy, clapping her hands together. She swallowed the last of an Oreo. "Any club business? Anything urgent?"

"The treasury's low," spoke up Dawn.

"How'd it get low?" asked Kristy.

"Mostly paying Charlie to drive you to and from the meetings."

"Well, dues day is coming up," said Kristy.

We all kick in some money from our babysitting jobs to keep our club running. We use the money to pay Charlie, to buy stuff for a slumber party or something every now and then, and to buy things to put in our Kid-Kits. (Kristy thought up Kid-Kits. They're boxes full of games and books — our old ones — plus new coloring books, activity books, and sticker books which we sometimes take with us when we sit.)

"One day of dues isn't going to do it," said Dawn worriedly.

"Well," Kristy went on slowly, "could all of you kick in double next time — just this once?"

We grumbled but agreed to. Nobody wanted to pay double, but we could afford it, since we earn so much money sitting.

The phone rang then and Claudia answered it and lined up a job for Dawn.

"Any other business?" asked Kristy.

Mallory and I glanced at each other. We had decided that we should talk more at the meetings — at least about business. At first we had wanted to keep a low profile; now we were worried that we weren't joining in enough.

I can't believe what I did next. I actually raised my hand — like some dumb firstgrader.

"Yes?" said Kristy, looking surprised. (About the hand-raising, I guess.)

"Well, I — I — I mean, I, um . . . um — "

Luckily the phone rang again.

I stopped talking as Mary Anne reached for the receiver and lined up a job for Kristy. As soon as Mary Anne was done, Kristy said, "Yes, Jessi?"

This time I managed to speak like a human. I thought the club members should know about Matt and his progress, since any one of them might baby-sit for him and Haley sometime. I told them that Matt and Haley were both making friends. Then I told them about the conversation Haley and I had had about what it was like to be Matt's big sister. Finally I said, "Is anyone interested in learning more about signing?"

I was surprised at the answer. "Yes!" chorused Kristy, Claudia, Dawn, Mary Anne, and Mallory.

"You *are?*"

"Sure," replied Claudia. "All the kids around here are learning to sign. We better learn how, too. Besides, us baby-sitters have to be prepared for anything."

"Right," agreed Kristy, who sounded as if she wished *she'd* said that.

So in between phone calls I showed the other club members how to finger spell. I figured that would be helpful because if they were sitting at the Braddocks and didn't know the sign for something, they could always spell the word out. (Finger spelling is somehow more personal than writing stuff on paper. At least you can *look* at the person you're talking to.)

We were up to the letter J when the phone rang. Dawn answered it, listened for a moment, and then put her hand over the mouthpiece and said with a grin, "Hey, Mary Anne, it's *Logan!*"

(Logan is one of our associate club members, but he's also Mary Anne's boyfriend, remember?)

Mary Anne took the receiver, faced herself into a corner of the room, and began talking so quietly that none of us could hear her, no matter how far we leaned over. Every so often a little murmur would come from her direction, but no actual words.

When she finally hung up, she turned back to us, blushing, and said, "Logan says hello. He just wanted to know what was going on. He said he might want a signing lesson sometime, Jessi. In case he ever sits for the Braddocks."

"What *else* did he say?" Claudia teased, looking at Mary Anne's red face.

(I feel sorry for anyone who blushes so easily.)

"Oh . . . not much."

We started talking about our families then. We do that sometimes, when we're not lining up jobs or talking about club business. We sort of take turns saying what's going on in our lives.

"My brother called from California last night," said Dawn. "He's still really happy out there."

"You think he'll stay?" asked Kristy.

"I'm pretty sure. When the six months are up, the lawyers and everyone have to get together again to discuss the trial period — but I know he'll stay."

I couldn't imagine my family being torn in half like Dawn's had been. I just couldn't. What would I do if Squirt and Daddy were living in California?

"Tigger learned how to fetch yesterday," said Mary Anne. "Have you ever known a kitten that could fetch?"

"You're just trying to distract us from Logan," said Dawn with a smile.

"You're absolutely right," agreed Mary Anne.

"Well, here's something that's been going on at my house," said Kristy. "I find this hard to believe, but Mom has been mooning around saying she wants a baby."

"A *baby?!*" the rest of us shrieked.

Kristy nodded, looking puzzled.

"Is she pregnant?" asked Claudia.

"Nope," said Kristy. "I know that for a fact because she's also been saying she wishes she were pregnant, but she thinks she's too old. After all, Charlie is seventeen."

"Yeah, but how old's your mom?" asked Dawn.

"I don't know. Thirty-seven or something."

"Then she could still get pregnant."

"Really?"

"Sure."

"Hmm."

Ring-ring.

"Hey, one of you guys want to get the phone?" asked Kristy, looking down at Mal and me.

"Sure!" we cried. We both leaped up.

"Only one of you can answer it," said Claudia. "Trust me. In the old days, the four of us always used to try answering the phone at the same time and it never worked."

I might be more agile than Mal, but she'd been sitting closer to the phone, so she reached it before I did. I plopped back down on the floor with a disappointed "Hmphh."

"Hello, Baby-sitters Club," said Mal professionally. She sounded good and she knew it. "Oh, yes. Hi, Mrs. Braddock. . . . Tell her what? . . . Oh, okay. Sure. . . . 'Bye."

Mallory hung up the phone and turned to

me quizzically. "That was Matt's mother. She said to give you a message: Everything is arranged."

"It is?!" I cried. "Oh, that's great. Really great!"

"Are you going to let us in on this?" asked Kristy.

"Yeah," said Mary Anne. "What's arranged?"

I hesitated. "I can't tell you. I mean, I can't tell you yet. But I'll be able to soon. . . . Really, I promise," I added when I saw their frowning faces.

"How come you can't tell us now?" asked Mal.

"I just can't, that's all. But I do want to ask you something — all of you. I was wondering if you'd like to come see *Coppélia*. Everyone in the cast gets ten free tickets to opening night, so I'm inviting Mama, Daddy, Becca, Grandma, Grandpa, and you guys."

The club members began shrieking, "Opening night! . . . The ballet! . . . Going to Stamford!"

I'd never heard them so excited.

I took their reaction as a yes.

CHAPTER 12

My personal feeling about the principal's office is that it's better not to be in it. For any reason. What could happen is that someone passes the office, sees you there, and spreads rumors about your being in big trouble, when in fact you're just handing in a late insurance form or something.

Despite my thoughts, I had to go to the principal's office early one Thursday afternoon. I had a note from my mother giving me permission to leave Stoneybrook Middle School an hour early that afternoon. When the school secretary read Mama's note and saw why I was leaving early, she started gushing. "Oh, what a lovely thing to do! Why, I think that's wonderful. Simply wonderful." She made out a pass and handed it to me saying, "You kids today! You're so nice and thoughtful. No one gives you enough credit."

I had to agree with her on that one.

At 1:25 that afternoon I was waiting on the sidewalk in front of school. At 1:30, Mrs. Braddock pulled to a stop in front of me, and I climbed into the front seat.

"Ready?" she asked, smiling.

"Ready as I'll ever be." I began rehearsing a speech with my hands. "What's the sign for costume?" I asked. I realized that this was not a good question to ask a person whose hands were gripping the steering wheel of the car you were riding in, but I asked anyway.

"I'll demonstrate at the next red light," Mrs. Braddock replied. And she did.

The ride into Stamford took awhile, and we talked and rehearsed the entire time. At last we were driving into the city. Tall buildings everywhere. I recognized the street my ballet school is on, and the street Daddy's office building is on. Finally we pulled into a parking lot with a big sign in front that said PARKING FOR SCHOOL FOR THE DEAF. We found a space and parked, and then Mrs. Braddock led me inside an old, old building that looked like it might once have been a mansion, somebody's home.

"It's run pretty much like any other school," Mrs. Braddock said as we walked slowly down a brightly lit corridor. "The kids go to art lessons and gym classes. They eat in a cafeteria.

The differences are that the classes are quite small — usually not more than eight students, at least in the lower grades, and that the children start here at a very young age. Matt was two when he entered, and the teachers began lessons in signing right away. His classes were much more intense than regular nursery school classes."

We were walking slowly because I kept trying to peek into classrooms each time we passed a doorway.

"The younger classes are on this floor," said Mrs. Braddock. "Matt's is at the very end of the corridor."

We reached the last door in the hallway and paused beside it.

"This is one of the two second-grade classes," Mrs. Braddock told me. "The children here are all seven years old, but they have different degrees of hearing difficulty. Some are profoundly deaf, like Matt. A few have some hearing. Several of them can speak. The children receive lots of individual attention. They all know how to sign, but those with speech are also given speech lessons. A few are learning lipreading. Matt may try that when he's older, if he wants to."

I nodded, trying to peek into the classroom.

"Since some of the children can hear, and

some are learning speech and lipreading," Mrs. Braddock went on, "make sure you speak — slowly and loudly — while you're signing, okay?"

"Right," I replied. (Mrs. Braddock had mentioned that before.)

"Well . . . are you ready, Jessi?"

"I hope so."

"Don't be too nervous. It's just a bunch of seven-year-olds who *love* visitors. And Matt's teacher and I will help you if you need it."

"Okay." I took a deep breath and let it out slowly, just like I do before I go onstage during a performance.

Mrs. Braddock opened the door and I entered Matt's classroom. Eight excited little faces turned to me, and a young woman rushed over to us.

"Hello, Mrs. Braddock," she said, shaking her hand. Then she turned to me and shook my hand. "You must be Jessi. I'm Ms. Frank, Matt's teacher. Thank you so much for coming. I'm glad this visit could be arranged." (This visit was what Mrs. Braddock's mysterious phone call had been about at our club meeting.) "The children are thrilled, even though they don't know why you're here. All I've said is that you have a surprise for them. Before I introduce you, though, I just want to say that your idea is marvelous. It'll be a great experience for the children, and I really want to thank you."

I was beaming. Everyone, at least once in his or her life, deserves such praise.

The children were still looking at me eagerly. You might have thought that eight deaf children would make for a pretty quiet class, but no way. First of all, the talkers Mrs. Braddock had mentioned were talking — loudly. (Matt's mother had said that since deaf children can't always hear themselves, they don't know how loudly they're speaking and have to learn to modulate their voices.) Some of the others made sounds as they signed to each other. And one child, finishing up an assignment, was listening to a cassette at top volume.

While Ms. Frank gathered the children into a circle on the floor, I took a quick look around. Matt's classroom seemed pretty much like a classroom in any elementary school, except that I felt bombarded by all the things there were to *see*. I guessed that Ms. Frank's idea was that if her kids couldn't learn by hearing, they'd learn by seeing. Every inch of wall space and table space was covered — with displays about the months of the year, telling time, using money, colors and shapes, insects and animals, you name it. Across the top of the blackboard was a long chart showing the alphabet. Underneath it was the finger spelling alphabet, a hand demonstrating each letter.

The other difference between Matt's room and most second-grade classrooms was the audio equipment — tons of headphones and tapes for the kids who could hear and talk.

Mrs. Braddock took a seat in the back of the room, and Ms. Frank led me to the front of the room.

"Why don't you sit on the floor with the kids?" she suggested. "You'll all feel more at ease."

(Good thing I was wearing jeans.)

Ms. Frank, also wearing pants, sat right down on the floor next to me. (Now that's my kind of teacher.)

"Boys and girls," Ms. Frank said, speaking loudly and clearly, and always facing the kids (so the lip-readers could watch her mouth), "this is Jessi Ramsey." She signed as she spoke, and of course spelled out my name, J-E-S-S-I R-A-M-S-E-Y.

Matt took his eyes off Ms. Frank's hands long enough to grin at me. I smiled back.

"Jessi is here," Ms. Frank went on, "because she knows Matt Braddock and has a very special surprise for you. Jessi?"

"Thanks," I said. Then I began speaking and signing. Ms. Frank stayed where she was, in case I needed help. "I am a dancer," I began. Then I finger spelled the word *ballet*, for which I hadn't been able to find a sign. "I like dancing because I can tell a story with my body. I don't need to talk."

A few faces perked up at this idea.

"A ballet," I went on, "tells a story without any words — just dance and music. I know some of you can't hear music, but did you know that you can feel it?"

The children nodded.

"We've talked about that," Ms. Frank told me. "We've been experimenting with vibrations — with rhythm and drumbeats and the piano."

"Oh, good." I began signing and talking again. "My dance school," I said, "is going to perform a ballet called *Coppélia*." (More finger spelling.) "I'll be dancing in it. It's about a toymaker and a big doll that he creates. Everyone will wear costumes — " (luckily I remembered the sign for that word that Mrs. Braddock had shown me in the car) " — and the stage will look like a village."

The children were hanging on my every word and sign.

"I would very much like for you to come see *Coppélia*, to come to the theater." (The invitation was for opening night, but I decided not to try to explain what that meant.) "I know you might not be able to hear the music, but you can watch the dancers tell their story. Do you want to come?"

"Yes! Yes!" cried the kids who could speak. The others nodded eagerly. Matt was so excited he looked like he might explode.

Ms. Frank spoke up then. "The story of *Coppélia* is a little complicated," she told Matt and his classmates, "so I'll tell it to you before you go to the show. Some of you might want to read about the story, too."

The boy sitting next to Matt raised his hand. "When is the show?" he signed.

"Next Friday," I told him with Ms. Frank's help. "Eight days from now."

"What should we wear?" signed another boy, and everyone laughed.

"Whatever you want," I told him, "but it might be fun to get dressed up."

The school bell rang for the end of the day, and I noticed that a big light flashed next to the door. I guessed that was the signal for the kids who couldn't hear the bell.

Even though school was over, none of the kids got up. Two more had questions. Finally Ms. Frank had to send them on their way. Soon the classroom was empty except for Ms. Frank, Mrs. Braddock, Matt, and me. While the adults were having some important-looking conversation, Matt showed me his desk and cubby and something (I wasn't sure what) that he'd made in art class.

I oohed and ahhed. And smiled a lot.

Then — quite suddenly — Matt threw his arms around me and gave me a big hug. He leaned back and signed, "I love you. I can't wait to see a ballet. Thank you. You're my best grown-up friend."

At first I wasn't sure what to react to — Matt's enthusiasm or being called a grown-up. It didn't take long to decide. I signed back, "I love you, too."

CHAPTER 13

Hey, everybody, Jessi's brother and sister are adorable! Especially Squirt. I mean -- not that Becca isn't cute, but Squirt is a baby after all, and there's something about babies..... Oh, well.

Anyway, while Jessi was at the Braddocks' I had a great time sitting at her house. I love taking care of babies, and Becca was a lot of fun. We had a good talk, too.

Then Charlotte Johanssen came over to play and suddenly I got the feeling that something was going on. Becca and Charlotte have a secret. But they wouldn't say a word about it. What's going on?

117

When Kristy baby-sat for Becca and Squirt, it was the first time she'd been over to my house — at least, the first time she'd been there since Stacey McGill moved out of it. She went over after school to watch my brother and sister while Mama went to Stamford to run boring errands that Becca and Squirt wouldn't want to be dragged along on.

When Mama left, Squirt was taking a nap, but Becca was bouncing around. She loves new baby-sitters because she can show off all her stuff to them, stuff the rest of us have seen a billion times. The first thing she showed Kristy was her rock collection. Now let me set you straight about something. What Becca knows about rocks and minerals you could fit on the head of a pin. She doesn't know shale from quartz. She just collects rocks she thinks are interesting. For example, she has a flat pebble that is almost exactly round and has a yellow splotch in the middle so that it looks sort of like a fried egg. And she has a rock that looks exactly like Mr. Millikan's nose. Mr. Millikan is the principal of the school Becca went to in New Jersey. The resemblance of the rock to his nose is really amazing. In Oakley, if you asked *any*body what that rock looked like, they'd say right away, "Millikan's nose." Here in Stoneybrook, people just say, "A nose?"

When Becca had shown Kristy every last one of the rocks, she moved on to her dolls and then her stuffed animals. Becca has so many of both, that when she sleeps with all of them, sometimes it's hard to pick Becca out of the crowd.

"Want to see my books about cats?" Becca asked Kristy next. "I have *The Christmas Day Kitten* and *Pinky Pye* and *Millions of Cats* and — "

"Bloo-ga!" Squirt suddenly called from his room.

"Oops! There's your brother!" said Kristy. I'm sure she was relieved that she didn't have to look at another collection. "Let's go get him up."

"Yeah!" cried Becca.

Kristy and Becca opened the door to Squirt's room, where their noses were met by baby smells — powder and Baby-Wipes and a wet diaper.

"Oh, you need to be changed," said Kristy, bending over the crib and feeling Squirt's diaper.

Squirt burst into tears. He wasn't expecting

a strange face to peer over the side of his crib. He was expecting Mama or Daddy or Becca or me.

Becca was pulling up Squirt's shade and opening the curtains.

"Hey, Becca. Come here," Kristy said. "Show Squirt your face."

Becca obliged and Squirt stopped crying. "Ga-ga?" he asked.

"I think that means he wants milk," said Becca.

Kristy dressed Squirt, and she and Becca and the baby went downstairs and all had some milk.

As they were sitting around the table (well, Squirt wasn't at the table; he was in his high chair, gumming up some crackers), Becca looked at Kristy and said, "You're really nice."

"Thanks!" replied Kristy, flattered.

"And I mean *really* nice. Not fake nice. Nice like you mean it."

"Of course I mean it."

"Some people don't."

"Who doesn't?" Kristy wanted to know.

"A lot of people in Stoneybrook. When we first moved here, either no one would play with me or people just pretended to like me."

Ah, thought Kristy. She knew what was coming. I've talked with the girls in the Baby-sitters Club about being black and trying to fit in in Stoneybrook. It hasn't been easy.

"Some people," Becca went on, "were just plain mean. Other people pretended to be nice, but they really weren't. . . . I don't know why they bothered pretending."

"You know what?" said Kristy. "Everyone has trouble fitting in sometimes."

"Everyone?"

"Everyone. You know Matt? The boy your sister is sitting for now?"

"The deaf one?" asked Becca.

"Yeah. Well, at first the kids in his new neighborhood didn't like him because he's deaf. And last summer I moved to a new neighborhood where no one liked *me*."

"Didn't like *you*?" Becca repeated, mystified. "But there's nothing wrong with you. I mean, you're not deaf or anything. And you're white."

"But I'm not rich. My mother married this millionaire and he moved Mom and my brothers and me into his mansion on the other side of town. The kids all knew where I'd come from, and they made fun of me. . . . Of course, I didn't help things by calling them snobs. But what I'm saying is that everyone is the odd one out sometimes. You're the only one in jeans at a fancy party, or the only Japanese kid in school, or the only diabetic in your class. See?"

"Yeah. Being called names still hurts, though."

"Oh, tell me about it. But doesn't it help to know that you're not the only one who doesn't fit in sometimes?"

"A scootch. It helps a scootch."

"I guess a scootch is better than nothing," said Kristy, and she and Becca grinned at each other.

"Kristy, can I invite Charlotte over?" asked Becca.

"Charlotte Johanssen? Sure."

"Oh, goody," said Becca, and she made a dash for the phone.

Charlotte is a kid the club sits for a lot. She's exactly Becca's age, but she's a year ahead of her in school since she's really smart and skipped third grade last year. Charlotte's favorite sitter used to be Stacey McGill, and she was crushed when Stacey moved away. In fact, it even used to be hard for her to come play with Becca, knowing she was in Stacey's old house. Luckily, she got over that, because Becca needs friends desperately. Charlotte was the first kid who didn't automatically avoid her or tease her just because she's black. She didn't seem to notice or care.

Becca and Charlotte were slowly getting to be good friends when something happened that totally cemented their relationship — the Little Miss Stoneybrook pageant, which was a sort of beauty show for little girls. Becca refused to be in it because she has terrible stage fright, and ordinarily Charlotte (who's on the shy side) wouldn't even have considered something like that. But she let herself get talked into being a contestant — and then blew it once the pageant started. She actually ran off the stage in tears and asked to be taken home.

Well, that did it. Becca sympathized completely. The two of them have been like Siamese twins ever since.

Kristy said that Charlotte reached our house less than five minutes after Becca called her.

"Hi, Kristy!" Charlotte said. (She isn't shy around the members of the Baby-sitters Club anymore.)

"Hi, Char. I'm glad you came over. What are you guys going to do?"

Becca and Charlotte looked at each other and raised their eyebrows.

"We're going to pretend we're ballerinas," said Becca. "Just like Jessi."

"Yeah," said Charlotte. "We're going to be the famous dancing team, the Polanski Sisters."

"We're going to dance in Jessi's practice area in the basement," Becca added.

"Is that okay with Jessi?" asked Kristy. "Are you sure you're allowed to do that?"

"Positive. She lets us all the time." (It's true. I do.) "Anyway, we have to rehearse for the big performance."

"What big performance?"

"The opening of *Copernicus*," replied Becca.

"*Coppélia*?" asked Kristy.

"Yeah, that."

"Okay. Just be careful with Jessi's things. Squirt and I will be playing upstairs."

"Okay!" Becca and Charlotte ran down to the basement.

Kristy looked at Squirt, who was an enormous mess. He had a milk mustache, and soggy cracker was everywhere — all over his face, in his hair, on his hands, covering the tray of his high chair.

It took Kristy quite awhile to clean him up, and after she'd finished, she realized his diaper was wet again.

How do parents do it? Kristy wondered. How do they run a house, take care of their kids, and go to work, too? It seemed impossible. She decided not to worry about it. At least not for several more years. Maybe by the time she was a parent there would be automatic diaper-changers or something.

When Squirt was clean and dry, she carried him down to the family room. She was going to show him some of his board books, but she decided to see what the girls were up to instead. She didn't hear a sound from the basement, which worried her.

Kristy stood with Squirt at the top of the steps. She could hear murmurings from the girls, but nothing more. She tiptoed downstairs. What *were* they doing?

"Becca? Char?" She found them sitting on one of Jessi's exercise mats. "What happened to the Polanski Sisters?" she asked.

Becca smiled. But she didn't answer the question. Instead she said, "We know a secret!" She didn't say it in a way that made Kristy cross. She said it as a point of interest, something she was excited about.

"Ooh, what?" asked Kristy.

"Can't tell." (Now *that* was annoying.)

"Can't tell *yet*," added Charlotte.

"You mean I'll find out?"

"Yup."

"When?"

"Can't tell." Becca and Charlotte grinned at each other. "But it's a good secret," said my sister.

Kristy remembered the mysterious phone

call I'd gotten from Mrs. Braddock. Something was going on. She knew that for sure. But what?

Kristy Thomas does not like to be left out of things.

CHAPTER 14

Opening night!

Oh, my lord!

I can't believe it!

The opening night of anything (if you're in the cast, that is) is the most exciting and also the most scary part of a production. It's even scarier than auditioning. Opening night is when you know whether your work has paid off. It's when you know whether you've worked hard enough. And it's the first time you perform your new role in front of a whole theater full of faces.

So I was nervous about the opening night of *Coppélia*.

But I wasn't *too* nervous. There have been other opening nights in my life, and there will be more. I hope.

This opening night would be special, though. It would be different from any other. This was because, thanks to the Braddocks,

Mme Noelle, and Ms. Frank, Matt and his class would be in the audience. That was part of the secret Becca had told Charlotte.

I'd kept the secret for as long as I could. I didn't hit the members of the Baby-sitters Club (even Mallory) with the news until two days before opening night. (Kristy canceled our regular Friday meeting on the afternoon of that first performance so that everyone could have time to get ready for the big trip to Stamford.)

The girls were really excited when I gave them the news.

"You did that for Matt?" asked Mary Anne with an awed smile.

"You *arranged* all that?" added Kristy.

I nodded.

Everyone looked impressed.

I felt great.

And now it was opening night. As I had promised, I'd given my ten free tickets to Mama, Daddy, Becca, Grandma and Grandpa (they'd traveled all the way from New Jersey just to see the show), and Kristy, Dawn, Mary Anne, Claudia, and Mal.

Guess who was going to baby-sit for Squirt? Logan Bruno, Mary Anne's boyfriend, one of the associate club members.

One other important person was also in the

audience — Mr. Braddock, Matt's father. Where were Mrs. Braddock and Haley? That's the rest of the secret, and you'll find out about it soon enough.

The performance was to start at eight o'clock. Now it was ten minutes to eight. My stomach was jumping around as if I'd swallowed grasshoppers. When the curtain rises on this ballet, Coppélia herself is already onstage. Dr. Coppelius has seated her on the balcony of his workshop. I, Swanilda, am the first to actually enter the stage.

But tonight — and only tonight — I would be onstage *before* the curtain rose.

Now it was five minutes to eight. My hair was fixed, my costume was on, my makeup was finished, I had shaken myself out and warmed myself up.

Five more minutes crawled by.

"Ready?" A hand touched my shoulder.

I jumped a mile.

"I am sorry," said Mme Noelle, "but it is time to begin. The house is packed. Oh, and your friends, the deaf children, they are sitting in the fourth row — center. Excellent seats."

"Oh, thank you so much, Madame," I said. "That's wonderful."

"Are you ready?"

"Yes. Yes, I am."

"All right then. Go ahead."

The audience had been noisy. They were chattering and rustling their programs and opening packages of candy. Suddenly they fell silent. I knew the lights had dimmed, the audience lights anyway. But the stage was still lit, and the curtain was down.

"Jessi?" asked another voice. It was Mrs. Braddock. She and Haley had appeared beside me, both very dressed up — and both very nervous.

"Okay," I said. I squeezed Haley's hand. "Let's go."

I was the first to walk onto the stage in the theater. I was followed by Haley and Mrs. Braddock. When we reached center stage, standing in front of the curtain, we stopped and looked out at the sea of faces.

"Good evening," I said, and Mrs. Braddock signed, "Good evening."

"Tonight's performance," I continued, "is a special one. In the audience are eight students from the school for the deaf here in Stamford." (Mrs. Braddock was still signing away — my translator.) "This," I said, "is Carolyn Braddock, the mother of one of the students, and Haley, his sister. So that the students can get as much as possible out of the performance,

Haley is going to narrate the story before each act and her mother will translate the narration into sign language. This is not usually part of a performance of *Coppélia*, but we hope you enjoy it anyway. Thank you."

I walked offstage then, to prepare for my real entrance, and behind me I could hear Haley speaking in a small, scared voice. "Louder!" I whispered, as soon as I was out of sight of the audience.

Haley spoke up. Her mother signed away. The audience liked them. I could tell.

The next thing I knew, the curtain was rising and the ballet was beginning for real. You might think that I was aware of the fact that my friends and family and Matt and his classmates were in the audience, watching me. But I wasn't. When I'm onstage, I *am* the dance. I'm the steps and turns and leaps. I'm Swanilda telling my story. Nothing less. For me, that's the only way to handle a performance.

Backstage, between acts, I paced around nervously.

"You are doing fine," Mme Noelle said to me several times. "A fine job."

Katie Beth, hearing Madame's praise, even added, "You really are. You're a perfect Swanilda."

131

I smiled and thanked her.

There was no way Swanilda could have been black, so I wasn't *perfect*, but I knew I was dancing very well. And I knew the show was going well. After all, we had rehearsed and rehearsed and rehearsed. It was paying off.

"You know something?" Katie Beth spoke up.

"What?"

"Adele's here tonight. She's in the audience. I told my parents about the special show, so we asked her to come home for the weekend."

"Hey, that's great!" I cried. "It really is. So the signing is for her, too."

"I think she wants to see you after the show. She really likes you. I mean because of the signing and tonight's performance and everything."

"I'd like to see her, too. Maybe she could meet Matt."

"Guess what. I'm learning how to sign," said Katie Beth. "There's a class at the school Matt goes to. I found out about it all by myself. Mom and Dad aren't taking it, but I started anyway. Adele is my only sister. She's not around much, but when she is, it'd be kind of nice for us to be able to talk like regular sisters do."

"That's great," I said again. "If you ever need any help, let me know. Better yet, maybe I should join the class. I might learn even faster."

"It meets on Mondays," said Katie Beth.

"Oh. That's a problem. I always baby-sit on Mondays. Well, anyway, I'm glad you're taking it."

Act II had ended and from the other side of the curtain I heard Haley say, now in a much more confident voice, "Act Three is the last act of the ballet. You will see the dancers in the village square again. Franz and Swanilda aren't mad at each other anymore, so they decide to get married, and they go to the Burgomaster for their dowries." (I had no idea how Mrs. Braddock was signing all this stuff, but I didn't bother to worry about it.) "But just then, Dr. Coppelius runs angrily into the square. He accuses Franz and Swanilda of wrecking Coppélia, which was his life's work. Since they did destroy the doll, Swanilda gives her dowry money to Dr. Coppelius. He is pleased by that, and after he leaves, Franz and Swanilda get married. And I guess they live happily ever after."

I smiled. Haley had added that last line herself.

Haley and Mrs. Braddock left the stage and the curtain rose. I became Swanilda again.

It's hard to describe how I feel when I'm onstage. But I think a bomb could have dropped and caved in the theater, and I'd still have been Swanilda, dancing.

I couldn't believe it when the final curtain came down. It felt as if no time had passed since I'd stood onstage with Haley and Mrs. Braddock. Yet I'd told Swanilda's story.

The audience was clapping loudly.

The cast assembled backstage. We held hands in a long line. When the curtain rose we stepped forward and bowed.

The audience clapped more loudly.

Christopher Gerber (who was playing Franz) and I let go of the people on either side of us and stepped forward to take our own bows. As we straightened up, I saw a figure climbing the steps to the stage.

It was Matt. His arms were full of roses. He walked timidly across the stage and handed them to me. Then he signed, "Thank you from all of us."

The audience had grown silent. I translated for them. Then, cradling the roses in one arm, I signed to Matt, "You're welcome. This is the best night of my life."

Matt signed, "Mine, too," and when I translated that, the audience laughed gently. Well, some people laughed. I heard a few sniffles, though, and saw a woman in the front row dig through her purse for Kleenex.

Matt turned to leave and Christopher and I stepped back into the line. That was when another figure, this one with flowing blonde hair, climbed the steps to the stage. The girl was also carrying flowers, a smaller bouquet, and was walking even more timidly than Matt had been.

It was Adele.

She stopped in front of Katie Beth and handed the flowers to her. Katie looked at her sister for a moment and both of them began to cry.

Oh, *no*, I thought.

But they recovered quickly. And Katie Beth said the last words I'd have expected her to say: "This is my sister, Adele. She's deaf, too."

I handed my flowers to Christopher in a rush, stepped over to Katie Beth, and translated what she'd just said into sign language. This was partly so Matt and his friends would know what was going on, but mostly so that Adele would know.

It was cause for more tears.

So I looked out at the audience and said, signing, "Any more flowers?"

Everyone began to laugh and the curtain came down. Applause rang in my ears. The show had been a success.

CHAPTER 15

The cast drifted offstage to change and to remove their makeup. We were elated — the show had gone very well — but we were also exhausted. I stayed behind with Katie Beth and Adele.

"I'm really glad you came," I signed to Adele. "I didn't know you were going to."

Katie Beth smiled at her sister.

"Surprise!" signed Adele. "I wanted to see you dance."

"She wanted to see us dance," I translated for Katie Beth, just in case she hadn't understood. I wasn't sure how much signing she'd learned.

"You never asked me to come to a show before," Adele went on, looking sad suddenly. "I thought you didn't want your friends to know me. You never even tried signing — until you met Jessi."

I translated for Katie Beth, who melted. The

sisters began to cry *again*. Before I left them alone, I said to Katie, "Tell her about the class you're taking. You know she'll be happy." And, I thought, then the two of them can cry some more.

For about five minutes, I had peace in the dressing room. I had just changed out of my costume and into my jeans and a sweater when — BOOM. Everyone piled backstage. And I mean everyone.

"Hi, honey!" That was Mama.

"Hi, babe!" That was Daddy.

"Hi, Jessi! Hi, Jessi!" That was Becca.

"Hello . . . hi . . . congratulations . . . fabulous show . . ." That was Grandma, Grandpa, Mr. and Mrs. Braddock, Haley, Kristy, Claudia, Dawn, and Mary Anne. Matt was there, too. He signed "congratulations" — a big grin as he clasped his hands in front of his face and shook them back and forth.

"Jess! I am so impressed!" *That* was Mal.

Everyone was standing around me in a bunch, but Mal pushed her way through the crowd and threw her arms around me.

I hugged her back.

"Do you know how glad I am that you're my best friend?" she said, pulling away and taking my hand. "I mean, not just because of this. You were already my best friend. But now you're a ballet star, too. That's amazing. I can't believe it!"

I grinned. "Thanks," I said. I didn't know what else to say, even though inside I *felt* lots of things to say. Sometimes I think I like ballet because it's easier for me to express myself with my body than with words.

Mal and I were still standing in that crowd when another voice spoke up. "Hi, Jessi," it said softly.

I must have been dreaming. I really must have. Had the whole evening been a dream? I guessed so, and felt disappointed.

The voice was Keisha's.

Just in case I wasn't dreaming, I turned around very slowly.

Keisha was standing behind me, smiling shyly.

"I don't believe it," I whispered. "I'm dreaming, right? This is a dream."

Keisha shook her head slowly. Then she glanced at Mal, and I realized that Mal and I were still holding hands. That awful guilty feeling came over me again.

Did Keisha think I'd betrayed her? I dropped Mal's hand.

"I came with Grandma and Grandpa," Keisha said. "Your parents sent me a ticket."

"Did you like the show?" I asked.

"It was wonderful. Your shows are always wonderful."

"Oh, Keisha," I said. And the next thing I knew, Keisha and I were hugging and crying. We were a reenactment of Katie Beth and Adele.

When we calmed down, I noticed that my family was smiling at me. How long had they been keeping the secret about Keisha's visit? I realized that there'd been a lot of secrets lately — getting Matt and his class to the performance, preparing Haley and Mrs. Braddock to take part in the show, Katie Beth and her signing class, and of course, Keisha's surprise.

Keisha and Mal and I stood around awkwardly.

"Are you Jessi's cousin?" Mal asked finally.

"Oh!" I exclaimed. "Sorry. I guess I should introduce you. Mal, this is my cousin Keisha from Oakley."

"The one who has the same birthday as you?"

I nodded. "And Keisha, this is Mallory. She . . ." I trailed off. How could I tell Keisha that Mal was my new best friend?

Mal saved the day. "I've heard a lot about you, Keisha. Jessi and I have tons of things in common, but not the same birthday. That's really special. I wish *I* had a cousin my age who was *my* best friend."

That did it. Keisha beamed.

Oh, thank you thank you thank you, I said silently, wishing I could send thought waves to Mal.

"Hey!" exclaimed Mal, "look who's here."

Matt had joined us. He signed that he had loved the ballet and so had his friends. But, he wanted to know, why were the men wearing stockings?

I translated for Mal and Keisha, who managed not to laugh. Then I tried to explain about ballet costumes, which wasn't easy.

"Honey," said my mother then, "we better get going. How would you like to go celebrate somewhere?"

"Like an ice-cream parlor?" I asked.

Mama laughed. "Or like a restaurant."

"Great," I said, even though I'd rather have gone out for ice cream. "Are we all going?"

"Every last one of us — if your friends call their parents to tell them they'll be home a little late."

"There's a pay phone out in the hall," I said.

My friends left, searching their purses for change on the way.

I was just putting on my coat when Adele and Katie Beth walked over to me. I introduced them to Keisha, signing.

From a little distance away, I saw Matt watching us. He ran to Adele when he saw her signing. Then they began signing away. They went so fast I couldn't follow them.

"Just when I think I'm really getting good," I said to Katie Beth, "I see deaf people who are *fluent* in sign language. Then I know how far I have to go."

Katie Beth nodded. "I feel like I've got miles to go before I catch up with *you*. . . . Listen, Jessi, I want to, um, to tell you s-something," she stammered.

I glanced at Keisha, who took the hint. "I better put my coat on," she said in a rush. "I'll see you in a few minutes." She hurried off.

"What is it?" I asked.

"You were — you were good tonight, Jessi. Really good. I know Madame made the right decision when she picked you to be Swanilda. I was jealous before. But I've got to learn that not everyone can have the lead."

"If they did," I said, giggling, "there wouldn't be any story. Just a bunch of dancing Swanildas and a bunch of dancing Franzes — or whatever you'd call more than one Franz."

Katie Beth giggled, too.

"You know," I told her. "I'll confess something. I know this sounds sort of, um, goody-goody, but when I was rehearsing Swanilda's role, part of me felt really happy and another part felt really guilty."

"Guilty? Why?" asked Katie Beth.

"Because since *I* got to be Swanilda, no one else did. I felt terrible about that. Isn't that weird?"

"I think it's nice. Goody-goody, maybe, but nice."

Katie Beth and I laughed.

Then we heard someone calling her name.

"Oh," said Katie Beth. "That's my mom. Adele and I better go."

"Okay," I replied as Katie Beth snagged her sister.

Adele and Matt waved to each other.

Then *my* mother was calling. "Jessi, let's get a move on. Everyone is ready to go."

Mama, Daddy, Becca, me, Grandma, Grandpa, Keisha, Mal, Kristy, Dawn, Mary Anne, Claudia, Mr. and Mrs. Braddock, Matt, and Haley climbed into four cars — the Braddocks', my grandparents', Mama's, and Daddy's. We drove to this place called Good-Time Charley's, which was sort of a compromise on the restaurant/ice-cream parlor question. It was a place that served hamburgers, quiche, and salads, but was famous for its desserts. The adults told the kids we could order whatever we wanted.

"All *right!*" said Haley.

"I'll say," agreed Claudia, the junk-food nut. I bet she was hoping for a butterscotch sundae.

Since there were sixteen people, we had to sit at two tables. We managed to divide it up unevenly, though — the ten kids at one table, the six adults at another. I just love being in a restaurant and not sitting with the grownups.

When the waiter brought the menus around, all us kids looked at the food side for about half a second, then turned the menus over and looked at the desserts.

Claudia ran her finger down a column, stopped abruptly, and said, "That's it! A butterscotch sundae!"

It took me awhile to choose something. When I'm dancing in a show I really watch what I eat. I was dying for cherry cheesecake, but I ordered ambrosia instead. Ambrosia is sliced-up fruit with coconut on it. I asked the waiter for whipped cream with it, though. I didn't want to be a total nerd.

"Boy," said Kristy when our food arrived,

"what a treat. This has been a great evening. I wasn't sure I'd like ballet, but I did. I especially liked seeing you, Jessi."

"Thanks," I said.

Claudia began smushing her sundae around. She likes to mix it up thoroughly before she eats it.

"Claudia, that is so gross," said Mary Anne. She glanced at Matt. "Is there a sign in the secret language for 'gross'?" she wondered.

"There's one for 'grotesque,' " I said.

"And for 'disgusting,' " added Haley. She made the sign, looking as if she were about to puke or something.

Matt looked at her in alarm.

Haley giggled, then tried to explain what we were talking about.

Matt just shook his head. He glanced around at all of us, with our sundaes and cakes and shakes and ambrosias. Then he patted his hand over his heart.

"Happy," he signed. "Very happy."

About the Author

ANN M. MARTIN did *a lot* of baby-sitting when she was growing up in Princeton, New Jersey. Now her favorite baby-sitting charge is her cat, Mouse, who lives with her in her Manhattan apartment.

Ann Martin's Apple Paperbacks are *Bummer Summer, Inside Out, Stage Fright, Me and Katie (the Pest)*, and all the other books in the Baby-sitters Club series.

She is a former editor of books for children, and was graduated from Smith College. She likes ice cream, the beach, and *I Love Lucy*; and she hates to cook.

Look for #17

MARY ANNE'S BAD-LUCK MYSTERY

My fear returned.

With shaking hands I lifted the lid of the box.

All I could see was tissue paper.

"Claudia? Do you have any tweezers?" I asked. "I'm not touching this."

"Oh, for heaven's sake." Claudia took the box from me and pulled the tissue paper up. She crumpled it into a ball, which she dropped on the bed.

"Ew!" shrieked Dawn, jumping away from the paper, and the rest of us screamed, too.

When we calmed down, we dared — all six of us — to peer into the box.

"What is it?" asked Mallory.

"It looks like a necklace," I replied.

Lying in the box was a tiny glass ball on a delicate gold chain. The ball was hollow, and inside was what looked like a seed — a small, blah, yellowish-brown thing.

I lifted the necklace out, afraid that at any moment it might go up in a puff of smoke, or that *we* might go up in a puff of smoke.

"Hey, here's a note!" I exclaimed.

"Oh, brother. Which one of us is going to read it?" asked Dawn.

"I — I guess I better," I said. "I mean, Kristy's right. The box was mostly addressed to me."

I dropped the necklace on the bed (everyone scrambled away from it), and opened up the note.

"Handwriting?" asked Kristy.

I shook my head. "Nope. More cutout letters from the newspaper."

"So what does it say?" asked Claudia.

"It — it says," I replied shakily, "well, see for yourselves."

I spread open the note on Claudia's bed. The members of the Baby-sitters Club leaned over to look at it, although I noticed that nobody got too close.

The note said: HALLOWEEN IS COMING. BEWARE OF EVIL FORCES. WEAR THIS BAD-LUCK CHARM, MARY ANNE — OR ELSE.

Here's some news about other books in The Baby-sitters Club series by Ann M. Martin

#1 *Kristy's Great idea*

Kristy thinks the Baby-sitters Club is a great idea. She and her friends Claudia, Stacey, and Mary Anne all love taking care of kids. But nobody counted on crank calls, wild pets, and uncontrollable two-year-olds! Having a Baby-sitters Club isn't easy, but Kristy and her friends won't give up till they get it right!

#2 *Claudia and the Phantom Phone Calls*

Claudia has been getting some mysterious phone calls when she's out baby-sitting. Could they be from the Phantom Jewel Thief who's operating in the area? Claudia has always liked *reading* mysteries, but she doesn't like it when they *happen* to her!

#3 *The Truth About Stacey*

The truth about Stacey is her parents want to find a miracle cure for her diabetes. They're making Stacey's life so hard! The other Baby-sitters are busy fighting The Baby-sitters Agency. How can they help Stacey and save the club, too?

#4 Mary Anne Saves the Day

Mary Anne's never been a leader of the Baby-sitters Club. Now there's a big fight among the four friends. It's bad enough when Mary Anne has to eat at the lunch table all alone. But when she has to baby-sit a sick child with no help from her friends — it's time to take charge!

#5 Dawn and the Impossible Three

Poor Dawn! It's not easy being the newest member of the Baby-sitters Club. She's got three impossible kids to take care of. And Kristy thinks things were better *without* Dawn around. It'll take a lot of work to make things run smoothly again, but Dawn's up to the challenge!

#6 Kristy's Big Day

It's a big day for Kristy, all right — she's a bridesmaid in her mother's wedding! And if that's not enough, she and the other Baby-sitters Club members have *fourteen* wedding-guest kids to take care of. Only the Baby-sitters Club could cope with this one!

#7 Claudia and Mean Janine

This summer the Baby-sitters Club is starting a play group in the neighborhood. Claudia can't wait for it to begin — it'll give her some time away from her mean big sister. But then her grandmother has a stroke . . . and the whole summer changes.

#8 Boy-Crazy Stacey

Who needs baby-sitting when there are boys around? Stacey and Mary Anne are mother's helpers at the Jersey shore, and Stacey's mind is on hunky lifeguard Scott. Mary Anne's doing the work of two baby-sitters . . . but how can she tell Stacey that Scott's too old, without breaking Stacey's heart?

#9 The Ghost at Dawn's House

Creaking stairs, noises behind the wall, a secret passage — there must be a ghost at Dawn's house! The Baby-sitters find themselves and one of their charges wrapped up in a mystery. Will they be able to solve it?

#10 *Logan Likes Mary Anne!*

Quiet, shy Mary Anne has been growing up lately . . . and the Baby-sitters aren't the only ones who've noticed. Logan Bruno likes Mary Anne! He has a dreamy southern accent, he's awfully cute — and he wants to join the Baby-sitters Club. Life in the club has never been this complicated — or this fun!

#11 *Kristy and the Snobs*

The kids in Kristy's new neighborhood aren't very friendly. In fact they're . . . well, snobs. They laugh at everything — even Kristy's poor old collie, Louie. Kristy's fighting mad. But if anyone can beat a Snob Attack, it's the Baby-sitters Club. And that's just what they're going to do!

#12 *Claudia and the New Girl*

Claudia really likes Ashley, the new girl at school. Ashley's the only one who takes Claudia seriously. Soon, Claudia's spending so much time with Ashley that she doesn't have time for baby-sitting — or her old friends. And they don't like it one bit!

#13 Good-bye Stacey, Good-bye

There are lots of tears when the Baby-sitters hear the news: Stacey and her family are moving back to New York. The club members can't think of a special enough way to send Stacey off. They want to give her much more than a party. But how do you say good-bye to your best friend?

#14 Hello, Mallory

Mallory Pike has always been good at baby-sitting her younger brothers and sisters. But is she good enough to join the Baby-sitters Club? The club members go overboard giving Mallory baby-sitting tests. Mallory's getting pretty fed up. . . . Maybe she'll just start a baby-sitting business of her own!

#15 Little Miss Stoneybrook . . . and Dawn

Mrs. Pike wants Dawn to help prepare Margo and Claire for the Little Miss Stoneybrook contest. And Dawn wants her charges to win! The only trouble is . . . Kristy, Mary Anne, and Claudia are helping Karen, Myriah, and Charlotte enter the contest, too. And nobody's sure where the competition is fiercer: at the pageant — or at the Baby-sitters Club!

#17 Mary Anne's Bad-Luck Mystery

Mary Anne finds a note in her mailbox. *"Wear this bad-luck charm,"* it says, *"OR ELSE."* Mary Anne's got to do what the note says. But who sent the charm? And why did they send it to Mary Anne? If the Baby-sitters don't solve this mystery soon, their bad luck might never stop!

#18 Stacey's Mistake

Stacey's so excited! She's invited her friends from the Baby-sitters Club down to New York City for a long weekend. But what a mistake! The Baby-sitters are *way* out of place in the big city. Does this mean Stacey can't be the Baby-sitters' friend anymore?